Gambler's Longshot

Devil's Knights Series

Book 5

Winter Travers

Natalie,

Thank you so m[uch] [for al]l
the love and su[ppor]t!
You're beyond amazing and I'm
so glad I found you the big
Indie World! Thanks for
taking a chance on me and
becoming not only a loyal
read, but also a friend!
Happy Reading!

Win Tra

Copyright © 2015 Winter Travers

ISBN-13: **978-1523375097**

ISBN-10: **1523375094**

Gambler's Longshot

Editor: Brandi Beers

Cover Designer: Winter Travers

For questions or comments about this book, please contact the author at wintertravers84@gmail.com

Cover Photos
Sula Strada © avanzimg

Passionate couple kissing © bezik

Dedication

For everyone who's taken a chance on a longshot and won.

Acknowledgments

My Boys. Thank you for being so understanding of my crazy ways. I love you both more than you know.

My Family. Thank you for all the support and love.

My Lester. Once a stranger, now my best friend. Thank you for being my ride or die and being a kick ass lady.

My Wicked Women. Ya'll rock. Best Street Team I could ask for.

My Beers Ladies. Love you three to death.

Chapter 1

GAMBLER

"I swear, woman, you need to get your ass back in that house, now!"

"And I swear, man, I don't know how many times I need to tell you, but you are not the god damn boss of me!"

That was it. I'd had enough. I had never met a woman more infuriating than Gwen. No matter what I told her, she threw it back at me, telling me to shove it up my ass.

"The damn cat will come back. There's no fucking point in traipsing all around the woods looking for it. It's two fucking o'clock in the morning." I continued following Gwen, pushing branches and brush out of the way.

"It's not just a cat, he's Mr. Tuna," she shot back at me. Like that made perfect sense. Don't even get me started on the ridiculous name she had given the cat. Half the time she called it Mr.T. Ridiculous.

"For Christ sake, Gwen, stop!" I yelled, grabbing her arm and ducked as a branch she had been holding back swung back, hitting me in the face.

She whirled around and stumbled into my arms and grabbed onto my shoulders. "I can't stop until I find Mr. Tuna. There is nothing you can say that will make me stop looking for him." She looked up at me, her eyes huge and doe-eyed. "That cat is all I have," she whispered, a lone tear sliding down her cheek. Gwen looked entirely different than when she is all dolled up at the salon. She still had the rock-a-billy look to her but softened. I was shocked when she had opened the door to me tonight. The tight white shorts that barely covered her ass and tight white tank top gave me a half chubby instantly.

Of course, as soon as she had opened her mouth and started bitching at me, my chubby friend deflated. Now with her soft, warm body pressed against me it had my chubby friend taking notice. Gwen was half a foot shorter than me, and I was always looking down into her doe eyes. Her eyes were something wet dreams were made of. She could convey so much with just her eyes.

Right now they were leaking tears and begging me to help her.

Son of a bitch, not tears. I could handle anything but tears. "He'll come back, doll."

"You don't know that. He could be lost and wandering around hurt. We need to find him," she pleaded.

"All right, we'll look for the damn cat, but can we please go back to the house for five minutes and put warmer clothes on?"

"Fine, but only for a minute, that's it." She pulled out of my arms and headed back towards the house.

Her firm ass taunted me the whole way, wagging in my face. She still had the tight shorts and tank on and managed to slip a pair of sandals on her feet as she dashed out the door after her damn cat. My boots were haphazardly pulled on my feet, the laces whipping around. Thankfully I hadn't gotten ready for bed yet and still had jeans and a tee on.

Just as we stepped onto the porch of her house, a motorcycle pulled into her driveway and killed the engine.

"Stay here," I grunted. I knew the only reason for Hammer to be here was not a good one.

"You lose your phone or something?" Ham called.

I patted my pocket where I usually kept my phone and felt nothing. "Shit, I left it in the house. I didn't have time to grab it." Just as I was getting ready for bed, Gwen had screamed bloody murder, and I hightailed it down the hall to see what the hell was going on. My only thought was to get to her and see if she needed help.

"Shits going down. You and Gwen need to get to the clubhouse now."

"What the hell do you mean?"

"Someone tried to fucking blow up Meg's house tonight."

"Holy shit," I groaned, running my fingers through my hair. There was only one person who would try to blow up Meg's house. The Assassins.

"Someone tried to hurt Meg?" Gwen called, panic in her voice.

"They tried, but they're all ok. King wants everyone at the clubhouse. Lockdown."

I nodded my head, knowing exactly what Ham meant. He cranked his bike back and headed back into town.

"We need to pack up and get to the clubhouse. Pack for at least a week, if not more," I ordered, marching up the steps, standing one step below Gwen.

"What? Why the hell for? I don't have anyone chasing after me. I can stay here. Plus, I'm not leaving until I find Mr. Tuna." She propped her hands on her hips, pure attitude.

"This isn't a fucking option, Gwen. Pack and we leave. The cat will be fine. It's an animal; it can survive outside."

"No way, no how. The only way I leave is if Mr. Tuna is with me." She glared at me.

"For fucks sake, we find the cat and then we leave, deal?"

She held her hand out to me, and we shook on it. "Deal."

"Get a can of cat food or tuna and let's find the little shit," I ordered. She ran into the house, the screen door slamming shut behind her.

I turned around, looking over her front yard and groaned. Of course, Gwen had to live out in the country. There wasn't a neighbor in sight, and she was surrounded by cornfields on one side and woods on the other. This was going to take all night.

I listened, trying to hear the little shit. Gwen came banging out of the front door, and I held my hand up, telling her to stop. She covered her mouth with her hand and whispered, "Do you hear him?"

"Quiet," I grunted. I heard the wind rushing around me, but I could also hear a soft meow. I kept listening, trying to figure out which way to go. I slowly walked around the back of the house, the meowing getting louder and louder.

Gwen was pressed to my back, one hand holding a can of tuna and the other gripping my arm. "I hear him," she whispered.

I looked around, trying to figure out where the hell he was. Thankfully the little shit was bright white and was easy to see in the dark. He was sitting at the back door, meowing to be let in.

"Mr. Tuna!" Gwen shouted, running around me and up the short steps to the back door. "I thought we'd never find you," she cooed, picking the cat up and cradled it to her chest.

They both acted like they hadn't seen each other in days when it had only been twenty minutes.

"You think we could continue this happy little reunion in the house while you pack a bag?"

"Don't mind him, Mr. Tuna. He's just a crab ass. He did help find you, though," Gwen cooed, rubbing her forehead against the cat's fur.

"We don't have time for this, Gwen. We found the cat, now pack."

"Dick," Gwen hissed as she whizzed by me, her precious cat tucked in her arms.

I followed behind, wondering what the hell I had done to deserve the sick and twisted punishment of Gwen Lawson. Lord help me.

'*'*'*'*'*'*'*'*'*'*'*'*

Chapter 2

Gwen

"What an ass," I vented to Mr. T, who laid on my bed, sprawled out on the pillow licking his paws.

I tossed my black crinoline skirt at the suitcase I had on the bed and walked back into my closet. Trying to pack when you had no idea how long you were going to be gone was hard. I needed to pack enough clothes for work and for whatever else we might do. Hopefully, Gambler would let me come back to my house to get more clothes if I needed them.

I grabbed three more skirts and four pairs of jeans and started folding everything to fit. I was going to need to bring two suitcases.

Mr. T pounced on my poofy skirt and rolled around, batting at it. I reached over, pulling him out of the tulle and cradled him to my chest. He meowed his protest of leaving the tulle cave and batted at my hand. "Don't you be an ass, too, Mr. T," I scolded, scratching him behind his ears. He purred, leaning into my hand, the tulle cave forgotten.

If only I could scratch Gambler behind his ear and do whatever I wanted. Right now, no matter what I said, he fought me tooth and nail about it. The same could be said about him, though. Ninety percent of the time I wanted to pop him in the nose and tell him to shove it where the sun doesn't shine.

I had never met a man that infuriated me so much. It had to do with the fact that the first time I had met him, he sauntered into my salon like he owned the place and told me what was going to happen and gave no room for argument. Ass.

"Doll, you about done? You've been packing for twenty minutes!" Gambler shouted through the door.

"I'll take another twenty minutes if I damn well feel like," I shouted back, flipping off the door. He couldn't see me, but it was satisfying none the less. Mr. T jumped from my arms and laid back down on my pillow.

I shut the first suitcase, tossed it on the floor and pulled another one out from under my bed. Now came the hard decision, shoes. I didn't want to leave any of my babies behind. I, Gwen Lawson, had a major shoe fetish. Heels were my utter weakness, but a cute pair of tennis shoes had been known to make me swoon a time or two.

"You got ten minutes, and we are leaving with or without all the shit you're packing," Gambler yelled. I heard him retreat down the hall, probably grabbing a beer from the fridge.

"Oh, hey!" I yelled, opening the door and peeked my head out. "Can you go down to the basement and grab Mr. T's carrier? He gets a little anxious on car rides if he's not in his carrier."

Gambler stopped walking and shook his head. He kept his back turn to me and mumbled under his breath. All I made out of it was a six pack of beer and General Tso's Chicken as he ran his fingers through his hair and headed in the direction of the basement.

I ducked back into my room, wondering if I should ever leave Mr.T with Gambler. I'd be afraid I'd come home to a homemade Chinese dinner and no more Mr.T.

"You are not eating my cat!" I yelled, opening the door and dashed down the hall to the basement door that was wide open. "Did you hear me?"

The light down in the basement was dim, and all I could see was Gambler's shadow wandering around looking for Mr. T's pet carrier. Just as I was about to tell him where to look for it, he walked over to the stairs, the carrier in hand.

"You done packing?" he gruffed, walking up the stairs.

"No, I still need to pick out shoes." I backed up as he neared the top of the stairs and bumped against the door.

"Easy, doll." Gambler grabbed my arm and steadied me. My eyes connected with his and I couldn't look away. This wasn't the first time this had happened to me. There was something about his deep, dark brown eyes that held me captive. I had never seen a brown so hypnotizing before.

"I should go pack my shoes," I mumbled but didn't move.

"Put some pants on too, doll. I don't want you going to the clubhouse looking like that."

"What?" I asked. Looking like what? I was in my freakin' pajamas which were just shorts and a tank top. Nothing scandalous.

"Trust me when I say this, doll. You walk into that clubhouse looking like that, I'm going to have to protect you from more than the Assassins. Every man in there who doesn't have an ol' lady will be all over you like white on rice."

"I'm in my pajamas and I don't even have any makeup on. You're crazy."

Gambler moved closer, his face inches away from mine. "You think because you ain't got makeup on that none of those guys will look at you?"

I nodded my head yes, unable to speak. Gambler's eyes were even more captivating up close. I was speechless. Speechlessness and I did not go together. There was always something to be said. Except now.

"When those guys lay their eyes on your plump, lush ass and perfect tits hanging out of that tank top, they aren't even going to make it to your face before they pin you against a wall and have their way with you."

"But…what… how would you know?" I whispered.

"Because I've been fighting the urge since I walked through that door tonight. You're lucky I'm a god damn gentleman. Otherwise, I'd have you bent over that kitchen table right now." He dropped the pet carrier at our feet and cupped my chin in his hand. "I need to know what you taste like," he growled.

"But you hate me," I breathed out, his lips hovering over mine.

"You got a smart mouth, doll, and I'd like to bend you over my knee for it, but I sure as hell don't hate you."

"Oh," I repeat. I was speechless.

His hand caressed my cheek, his other hand loosening his grip, not forcing me to stay, but I didn't want to move.

He brushed his lips against mine and, as much as I'd like to deny it, I moaned as his hand delved into my hair, his lips assaulting me. He wrapped his arm around my waist and pulled me to him, our bodies flush. I wrapped my arms around his neck and held on.

I heard him growl low in his throat as he deepened the kiss, his tongue taking over my mouth, taking everything and making me want more. I was so into the kiss, I swear I could hear AC/DC playing "Highway to Hell." Wait, "Highway to

Hell" was not the song I would imagine when kissing Gambler.

I backed away, pulling my lips away from Gambler and shook my head. I didn't hear it anymore and thought I must be going crazy.

"Get back here, doll," he growled, grabbing me by the neck, his lips claiming mine again. Just as I was about to get lost in Gambler again, "Highway to Hell" started playing again. "Stop," I said, pulling away. "Your phone is going off."

"Ignore it." He grabbed me by the waist, but I leaned back and pushed on his chest.

"No, that's, at least, the second time it's gone off. It might be important."

Gambler stopped pulling me to him and his eyes cleared of the lust that had turned them almost black. He shook his head and let me go. I stumbled back into the kitchen, somehow missing the feel of Gambler's arms wrapped around me. "Uh, sorry, doll. I shouldn't have done that," he mumbled, running his fingers through his jet black hair.

"Oh, ok," I whispered. I reached up, my fingertips brushing against my lips. I agree it probably wasn't the best time for Gambler to kiss me, but I definitely wouldn't fight him if he did it again.

His phone started blaring again from the table and we both stared at it.

"Go finish packing, we leave in ten minutes," he ordered, the first one snapping out of the daze our kiss had put us in.

I slowly walked back to my room, Gambler rumbling into his phone. I was almost to my room when he yelled,

"Make sure you change. You're not leaving this house looking like that."

I halted in my tracks, and I felt my blood boiled. I stomped my foot and stormed into my room, slamming the door behind me. Childish yes, but dammit did Gambler piss me off.

One minute ago I was putty in his hands, and now I was ready to rip his dick off and feed it to Mr. T.

He wanted me to change? I'll give him change.

''*'*'*'*'*'*'*'*'*'*'*

Chapter 3

GAMBLER

One hour.

It took her one fucking hour until she walked out of her bedroom and when she did my jaw hit the floor.

She walked out of her room looking like a nineteen fifties pin-up model. She had a low-cut black dress that her tits were about to fall out of and swayed around her perfectly toned legs. Her hair was curled and pinned up to her head and her makeup was perfectly applied. Don't even get me started on her shoes. I never knew a pair of shoes could scream 'fuck me' like her's did. She looked like she was ready to go out, not go to the clubhouse and go to sleep.

"I'm ready," she murmured, smoothing her skirt down.

"The question is what exactly are you ready for?"

She puffed her chest out and my eyes stayed glued to her chest, hopeful to get a glimpse at her tits if they popped out. "You're a dick."

"I've been called worse. Now tell me where the hell you think you are going looking like that?"

"To the clubhouse."

I shook my head and couldn't believe this woman. I knew she had done this just to spite me because I told her to change, but my reason for her changing was a damn good one. "This isn't a game, Gwen. I didn't tell you to change just to piss you off."

She rolled her eyes at me and walked back into her room. She walked back out with a coat thrown over her shoulders and two suitcases trailing behind her. "What the fuck did you pack? We're going to the clubhouse, not the damn jungle. You've probably got enough packed for a month."

"Doubtful. The small one is just shoes."

One of her suitcases was just shoes? Who the hell has that many shoes, let alone insists packing them. "How many pairs of shoes did you bring?"

"5 pairs of heels, 3 pairs of boots, 3 pairs of tennis shoes, and 6 pairs of flats. Oh, and three pairs of house shoes."

Gwen had just packed twenty pairs of shoes. Motherfucking twenty. "What the hell are house shoes?"

She rolled her eyes at me again, and I was ready to lay her over my knee and let her know what I thought of her attitude. "Slippers, Gambler."

"Then say fucking slippers." I grabbed the suitcases out of her hands and made my way down the hall. "You're gonna have to drive your car. I'll follow behind you. Just take it easy and everything should be fine."

"This is utterly ridiculous, Gambler. I don't even know why I'm being included in this lockdown business. No one is after me," she sassed, walking back into her room.

"Gwen, for fucks sake, can we get the hell out of here? I'm god damn tired!" I hollered, opening the door.

"Don't get your panties in a bunch, I just had to grab Mr.T and my purse." She tossed her bag at my chest, knocking the wind out of me with how heavy the fucking thing was.

"You got fucking rocks in here?" I picked her purse up off the floor and weighed it in my hand. The damn thing had to at least weigh ten pounds.

"No, dick. I have makeup and other important things in there."

"Like what?"

"None of your damn business, is what." She crammed Mr. T into the carrier and picked it up, the damn cat meowing in protest. "I got Mr. T, you grab the rest."

"Leave the cat and I'll grab him after I put this stuff in your car."

"I can carry something," she insisted.

"I never said you couldn't. Drop the cat and get your ass in the car." I was losing all patience.

"Do you think I'm some helpless girl who can't carry anything?" She popped her hip out and rested her hand on it. Pure fucking attitude.

"No, Gwen, I'm pretty sure you are anything but helpless, I was just trying to be god damn nice."

"I didn't ask you to be nice to me!" Why the fuck was she yelling at me? I was trying to be a gentleman and this is what it got me?

I wasn't going to take her fucking attitude anymore. "Get your ass in that car right now. You have five seconds before I throw you over my shoulder and we leave with what's only on your back. No clothes, shoes, or fucking cat. You got me?"

Gwen took a step back, her face paling. I didn't mean to yell at her, but fuck me. No matter what I did, she fought me. "Four seconds," I warned, taking a step towards her.

She squeaked as I took another step and set the cat down. She side stepped around me and dashed out the door.

I ran my fingers through my hair, wondering how the hell I was going to make it through sharing a room with this woman.

I heard her car door slam and knew she was waiting for me. I turned off all the lights and grabbed the cat carrier. I swung the door shut behind me, flipping the lock up before it shut.

I tucked the carrier under my arm and pulled the two suitcases behind me. "Pop the trunk," I hollered when I got to the front of her car. She drove a little Beetle that matched her to a T. It was pitch black, with blacked out wheels and tint. It wasn't a Beetle you saw every day. Just like everything else in Gwen's life, there was a definite edge to it.

She swung out of the car, walked around to the front and opened the trunk for me. "So you'll let me open the trunk for you, I see." She propped her hands on her hips and watched me toss the suitcases into the car.

"You want the cat in the front or back seat?" I asked, slamming the lid shut.

"I'm surprised you didn't try to shove him into the trunk."

"Front or back, doll?"

"Front," she huffed out as she slid back into the driver's seat and slammed the door shut.

I opened the passenger side door and set the cat down who had been meowing protests the whole time. Thank god I didn't have to be in the same car as the little shit. I probably would have thrown it out the window halfway to town.

"All right, take it slow and drive straight to the clubhouse. I'll be right behind you the whole time." Gwen stared straight ahead and didn't look at me. "You hear me?"

"Loud and clear, Gambler."

I slammed her door shut and shook my head. She started up her car and peeled out of the driveway, kicking up dust and gravel. Her taillights disappeared down the road as I jogged over to my bike and swung a leg over it. I cranked it up, thankful I had packed up my bag and put it in my saddlebags before.

I gunned it out of her driveway and drove like a bat out of hell trying to catch up with her. I caught up with her, the glow of her red taillights ten car lengths ahead of me. I honestly had no idea what the hell I was going to do with her. I knew I wanted to know what her heavenly body felt like underneath mine, but I didn't know if I would live through all the sass and attitude she threw at me all the time. I wasn't lying when I said I wanted to put her over my knee and spank the sass right out of her.

She rolled through the stop sign at the end of the road and squealed her tires, heading into town. Never mind me telling her to take it slow and make sure I'm behind her. I pulled through the stop sign, too, making sure no one was coming and rocketed after Gwen.

Gwen had just made up my mind what I was going to do with her. I had never met a woman before who could resist me. Be it a friend or lover, I could always win them over. After the kiss we had shared, I knew there was more to Gwen than what she showed. She came off as kick ass and tough, but I knew underneath all the rockabilly attitude, there was a woman I wanted to get to know.

And whether Gwen liked it or not, I was going to see what she was trying too hard to keep away from me.

''*'*'*'*'*'*'*'*'*'*'*'*

Chapter 4

Gwen

I was tired. Like, *drain*ed.

When we had finally made it to the clubhouse, only King, Troy, and Rigid were awake. Gambler had dropped my bags by the door and had told me he would be right back. That was forty-five minutes ago and my eyelids were heavy and my eyes scratchy. I was edging past tried, falling into exhaustion.

I was sprawled out on the couch with the T.V. muted, a late night infomercial playing. My whole plan of getting all dressed up and strutting into the clubhouse had been foiled by the fact the only guys who had seen my entrance were all in a relationship and had eyes only for their women.

"Let's go, doll. I'm dead on my feet."

I looked over the back of the couch and saw Gambler standing at the edge of the living room. "It's about time."

"Save the sass for the morning, doll. I don't have it in me to deal with it right now. I've been going since five o'clock yesterday morning."

"Ew, what an ungodly time to wake up," I groaned, standing up and pulling my two suitcases behind me.

Gambler grabbed one out of my hand and headed down the hall. "I had a bunch of shit to deal with over at the body shop."

We came to the end of the hall and took a left, passing three doors before he pulled his keys out of his pocket and opened the fourth door.

"It ain't much but it's mine," Gambler mumbled, pushing the door open.

I walked in, as he reached in and flicked the light switch on. He wasn't kidding when he said it wasn't much. There was a bed directly in front of me with a huge T.V. hanging on the wall to the left of the door. There was a dresser and a desk to the right and a closed door next to the bed. "Simplistic."

"Is that the nice way of saying boring?" Gambler laughed, pulling my suitcases in and setting Mr. T's cage on the bed. I pushed the door shut and walked over to Mr. T, who was meowing like crazy. He had dozed in his cage while I waited for Gambler, but he was wide awake now.

"It's not boring, just simple." I pulled Mr. T out of his cage and set him on the bed. He cautiously walked around the bed, his eyes round and big, wondering where the hell we were.

"Call it whatever you want, doll. I'm gonna hit the head, I'm ready for bed."

I looked around wondering where the hell Gambler was going to sleep. "Um, where exactly are you sleeping?" I asked as he opened the bathroom door.

He turned around and looked at me, a grin spreading across his lips. "Right there, doll." He pointed to the bed and my stomach dropped. Shit.

"OK, so where am I going to sleep?"

"Well," he grabbed the hem of his shirt and pulled it over his head and tossed it on the floor. "Right now your only options are the bed or the floor."

"This place is huge, there has to be another bed that I can sleep in."

"They're all full, doll. That is unless you want to share a bed with Hammer. I'm sure he won't mind you sneaking into his bed with him."

"I don't want to sleep with anyone, especially not Hammer. Can't you sleep on the floor, I thought you were a gentleman." I crossed my arms over my chest, unwilling to sleep with anyone. "Or, you can go and sleep with Hammer."

"Dream on, doll. My ass is going to be in that bed in less than two minutes. So you need to decide where the hell your head is going to lay tonight." He turned around, walked into the bathroom and swung the door shut behind him.

Shit. Fuck. Shit. I didn't want to sleep with Gambler tonight. Gah, why were the Gods against me tonight? First I couldn't control myself when Gambler kissed me, and now I was being forced to sleep with him. Not at all how I had planned my night going. I heard the toilet flush and the water turn on. I only had probably thirty seconds before Gambler walked in shirtless and possibly with no pants on.

I grabbed the empty pet carrier and set it next to the desk. I pulled my suitcase onto the bed and rummaged through it, trying to find my pajamas. I was going to have to sleep with Gambler. There was really no way around it. As much as I wanted to make him sleep on the floor, I knew I couldn't do that to him.

With my pajamas and makeup bag in hand, I waited at the bathroom door waiting for him to come out. I bent over, tucking my clothes under my arm and slid my heels off. Just as I got the second one off, Gambler walked out of the bathroom, my head level with his crotch. Just lovely.

"That's one way to greet someone when they walk out of the bathroom," he chuckled.

I stood up, almost smashing my head into his leg, and stood face to face with him. Well, it wasn't exactly face to face. It was more face to chest. Without my heels on I was much shorter than Gambler. "I was taking my shoes off."

"Sure," Gambler said, walking around me, "keep telling yourself that, doll."

I stormed into the bathroom and slammed the door shut behind. Fuck he was an infuriating man. I dropped my makeup bag on the side of the sink and looked in the mirror. My hair was still perfectly pinned and my makeup perfect, but I felt like I had been run over by a Mac truck. I grabbed a makeup wipe out of my bag and started erasing my hour worth of hard work.

After all my makeup was off, I unpinned my hair, dropping the discarded bobby pins into my makeup, a couple missing their target when I threw them, but I didn't pick up. Hopefully Gambler steps on them and wonders where the hell they came from.

I brushed out my hair, feeling the sleek smoothness under my fingers and grabbed my clothes off the back of the toilet.

I didn't really have conventional pajamas. Most of the time it was an old vintage tee and booty shorts. When Gambler had unexpectedly come over tonight, I was already dressed for bed and he got a glimpse of my shortest booty shorts. Hell, he saw me in them the whole time. His eyes flared when his gaze ran up and down my body. I knew what I was working with and how to flaunt it. I had a nice rack, thick thighs, and a nice ass. I had to say I think Gambler agreed. I had just recently dyed my hair a deep midnight blue that every time the sun or light hit it just right the dark blue shined.

I stepped out of my dress and hung it over the shower rod, deciding I would hang it up in the morning. As I slipped on my tee and shorts, my long day really hit me, and I felt like I was ready to fall over. After tossing my hair up in a messy knot on the top of my head, I turned off the light and opened the door to pitch dark.

"About time," I heard grumbled from the darkness.

"I was in there for ten minutes." If Gambler was grumbling about ten minutes, he was going to shit a brick when he saw how long it took me to get ready in the morning. "Why did you turn off the lights? I can't even see my hand in front of my face."

"Jesus," he mumbled. I heard him reach around and then his phone lit up the room. "Get your ass in bed, doll."

"Where's Mr. T?" I asked, looking around the floor for him.

"His fluffy ass is under the covers, purring like there's no tomorrow."

"You let him under the covers?" I was utterly shocked. From what I had seen of Gambler and Mr. T together, they weren't fans of each other

"He didn't really give me much choice. As soon as I pulled the covers back he sprang up on the bed and burrowed to the bottom of the bed."

I walked to the bed and pulled the covers back, Mr. T staring back at me. "Hey pretty man," I cooed.

"Jesus Christ, you did not just call the cat pretty man."

My eyes snapped to Gambler, "He's my cat, I'll call him whatever I want."

"You know what, I think we just need to stop talking to each other altogether. Although I'm sure you'd get pissed at me for breathing too loud then."

He was probably right. "You do breathe too loud."

Gambler rolled his eyes and shut the light off on his phone. "Sleep, now," he ordered.

I slipped under the warm comforter, laying on my side and Mr. T crawled to my bent knees and cuddled into me. I was facing Gambler but couldn't see him. "Why is it so dark in here?"

"Because it's night time, doll. That's what happens."

"I know that, dick. I meant why don't you have a night light on?"

"Do I look like a fucking five-year-old who needs a night light, doll?"

"No, it's just that I typically need some kind of light on to sleep." I always left a light on in my living room, plus I had a night light in the hallway and my bedroom. I may come off as a badass, but I still had stupid, irrational fears. Darkness was one of them.

"I know, whenever I slept at your house after you feel asleep I had to turn off all the god damn lights just to get some rest."

"Hey! You can't turn off my lights."

"Gwen."

"What?"

"Can we finish this argument in the morning? When I said I was exhausted, I meant it." I could hear how tired he was and I felt bad that I was keeping him awake.

"Yeah, I'm sorry," I whispered.

"Nothing to be sorry for, doll. I just need some sleep. I'm sure you do, too."

I opened my mouth to argue with him that I wasn't tired, but I stopped and realized I was tired too. What the hell was wrong with me? He was right, every time he said something to me I had to disagree with him, even if I was wrong. "Night, Gambler," I whispered.

"Night, doll." He rolled over, his back to me and his breathing even out within minutes, and I knew he was asleep.

Mr. T was purring contently cuddled up to me and I closed my eyes. Maybe I was ridiculous with Gambler. He never really did anything to me to warrant the attitude I threw at him all the time. He just drove me crazy. He was always telling me what to do. I think what really drove me crazy was he only told me what to do because he was trying to be nice.

I never had anyone who told me what to do who had my best interest at heart. I sighed, wondering what the hell was wrong with me. I finally had a guy who tried to be nice and treat me right and what did I do? Call him a dick all the time.

"Do I have to turn on the goddamn bathroom light so you will stop huffing and puffing over there?" Gambler growled.

"I thought you were sleeping?" I whispered. I didn't mean to wake him up.

"I'm not." Jeez, he sounded annoyed. "You want the light on or not?"

Um, I totally wanted the light on but I didn't want Gambler to go out of his way to make me happy. I decided not to say anything and prayed he would go back to sleep and I would try to get a handle on my sighing.

Gambler whipped the cover back, scaring both Mr.T and I, got out of bed and stalked over to the bathroom. The light flicked on, illuminating half the room. I turned over, catching a glimpse of his back that was heavily tattooed, as he pulled the door almost shut, leaving it open a crack. It was perfect. It didn't light up the whole room, but it helped to make the room not so dark.

He stomped back over to his side of the bed and slid back under the covers, tossing them over us. "Sleep," he growled.

Mr. T cuddled back up to me and was purring within seconds. I tucked my hands under my cheek and closed my eyes. I was out in minutes.

''*'*'*'*'*'*'*'*'*'*'*'*

GAMBLER

I heard light snoring and thanked God she was finally asleep. Gwen was always going a mile a minute, even while lying in bed trying to go to sleep. I could hear all the thoughts swirling around in her head before I turned on the bathroom light.

I was amazed she didn't put up more of a fight when I told her that she would have to sleep with me. I'm sure if she actually would have put up a fuss I could have found somewhere else to sleep, but I wasn't going to let her know that.

Turning over, I saw her beautiful face that was always throwing sass at me, finally relaxed and looked peaceful. Two weeks ago she had dyed her hair dark blue and somehow pulled it off. I had never met someone like her before that was always changing something about the way they look. Whether it was her hair, nails, makeup or clothes, you never knew what Gwen was going to look like every morning.

The only time I saw her not all gussied up was right before she went to bed or right when she woke up. She didn't stay relaxed and casual for long. Her clothes were some kind of armor for her. What she was protecting herself from I had no clue.

She talked about her aunt often, telling me she was the whole reason she had moved to Rockton. I didn't know much except her aunt had raised Gwen and her sister and she felt it was her job to take care of her now. The aunt had a stroke two months ago and was just recently getting back to normal. I had yet to meet her, but I knew it was only a matter of time that I would be able to.

Gwen went to see her at least three times a week, and I would be going with her this week since King wanted someone with each of the girls at all times.

She rolled over in her sleep, cuddling into me, resting her head on my shoulder. She sighed contently and continued to snore. I wrapped my arm around her, pulling her to me and kissed her on the top of her head.

I know I had told her after our kiss that it was a mistake, but I was wrong. Kissing her was probably one of the best choices I had made in a while.

She tossed her arm over my stomach, and I wondered what the tough chick who fought me at every turn would think about the sleepy, sweet Gwen, who was curled to me, sleeping peacefully.

I closed my eyes, willing sleep to come and pushing all thoughts of Gwen's soft, sexy body pressed against me out of my mind.

It took a long fucking time to fall asleep.

''*'*'*'*'*'*'*'*'*'*'*'*'*'*'*'*

Chapter 5

Gwen

"Holy shit, did you have to drug her to sleep in the same bed as you?"

"No, I just knocked her over the head and had my way with her."

"Ah, nice."

What the hell was I listening to? I cracked one eye open and looked right into Mr. T's eyes. He let out an 'I'm hungry' meow and batted his paw at me.

"I got some shit to take care of. You think you can hang out with Gwen for an hour or so?" Gambler asked, his footsteps sounding like they were headed out the door.

"Yeah, Troy and I were going to grab some breakfast. I'm sure Gwen will want to come with us." My brain unfogged a bit and realized Gambler was talking to Marley.

"Thanks. Just stay with Troy and don't let her out of your sight." The door slammed shut and there was quiet.

"I know you're awake, bitch."

Shit, I didn't think I moved at all. How the hell did she know I was awake? I had every intention of faking sleep so Marley would go away, and then I could actually go back to sleep. "It's all a figment of your imagination," I chanted, waving my arm back and forth.

"Hmm, so you sleeping with Gambler last night is also part of this figment of my imagination, too?" Marley grabbed the covers and pulled them off and tossed them on the floor.

"Yes, you're sleep walking. Go back to sleep, Marley, you're drunk."

Marley tossed her head back giggling and jumped on the bed. "How did I go from sleep walking to drunk?"

"Drunk sleepwalking. That explains it all. Now leave me, I need my beauty sleep." I grabbed Mr. T and cuddled him to me, burying my face in his fur.

"It's almost noon. You need to get your ass up and go to lunch with Troy and me. Plus, I need to fill you in on everything that happened with Troy last night."

"From the sounds of it, I would say things went well with Troy last night if that silly smile on your face is any indication."

"Oh, things went way more than well." Marley laid down next to me, grabbing Gambler's pillow and crammed it under her head. "Hmm, Gambler smells good," she said, burying her face in the soft pillow.

"I wouldn't know," I mumbled, lying. I totally knew how good Gambler smelled. I had woken up a couple of hours ago, surprised that I was wrapped around Gambler, my head resting on his bare chest.

"I bet you don't know," Marley laughed, tossing the pillow at me. "Up. Now." Marley rolled off the bed and stood up, straightening her clothes.

"You are such a bitch."

"No, I'm not. You're just pissed I walked in on you sleeping with Gambler."

"Whatever. You think we can swing by the shop after lunch?" I asked, running my fingers through my hair.

"Oh, I know that look!" Marley exclaimed, pointing her finger at me.

"What? What look?" What the hell was she talking about?

"The same look you got the last time you changed your hair. What are we going to do this time?" Marley clapped her hands, a smile lighting up her face.

"Um, maybe highlights?"

"Blonde?"

"Eh, been there."

"Blood red?" I could tell Marley was getting more and more excited with each guess.

"Nope."

"Purple? I don't know how well that will show up with the midnight blue you have right now." Marley bit her lip, studying my hair.

"I've done purple so many times. No purple."

"I give. Tell me," she ordered, propping her hands on her hips.

I grabbed a strand of hair and twirled it around my finger. I knew as soon as I say it, Marley was going to flip. I had been needing a change, but didn't know what I wanted to do. It had just popped into my head and I knew it was exactly what I needed. "Orange."

Marley's jaw dropped and I knew I had shocked her. "Wow. Like all over?"

"Kind of like peek-a-boo. Here and there, mostly underneath." I ran my fingers through my hair, feathering it out.

"Holy shit, I'm excited! Get up, let's go! I'd say let's skip lunch, but I know Troy is starving. You get dressed, I'm gonna go check on Meg." Marley dashed from the room, not waiting for a response.

I stretched out, Mr. T meowing in protest. I stood up, pulling my hair up into a messy knot on the top of my head and looked around the room.

It was just as plain as I thought it was last night, you couldn't even tell whose room it was. Right now it looked like I lived here, not Gambler. All my crap was spread out on the bathroom sink and my top suitcase was open, clothes hanging out of it.

Gambler really was a mystery to me. All I knew about him was the little he had told me and what I had picked up from being around him.

I grabbed my suitcase and threw it on the bed and unzipped it, clothes busting out of it. I really did have a shoe and clothing addiction. I couldn't help it. It was unbelievable what a fabulous pair of shoes paired with the perfect skirt could do to boost your mood.

I grabbed my cropped jeans, white button down shirt and a red bandana to tie my hair back with.

As I slipped on the jeans and shirt, I felt like I was channeling Rosie the Riveter from those magazine ads from the fifties. I grabbed a black pair of flats and slid my feet into them.

After fifteen minutes of quick swiping on eyeshadow and lip gloss, I tied my hair back with the bandana and grimaced. I had puffy bags under my eyes, and I just looked tired. I may have gotten seven hours of sleep, but you sure couldn't tell by looking at me.

I flipped the bathroom light off and grabbed my purse as I walked past Mr. T, who was sprawled out on top of the bed and gave him a quick pat on the head.

I quick set up his kitty litter, cursing myself for not doing it earlier. I'm surprised Mr. T wasn't crossing his legs, giving me the evil eye.

"Hey, you ready?" Marley asked, sticking her head in the room.

"Yeah, I just had to get Mr.T all set up." I grabbed my purse, hitching it up on my shoulder and slipped out the door, making sure it was shut behind me.

"Troy's waiting in the truck. I told him after lunch we were headed to the salon."

"I'm sure he was excited about that," I laughed, following Marley down the long hall and into the common room.

"Ha, you're right. I told him I would make it up to him later." Marley glanced back at me, winking.

No one was in the large common room, only the TV playing quietly, as we walked past. I had never seen this part of the clubhouse without someone in it. "Where is everyone?"

"The guys are in church and Meg and Cyn are in Lo's room watching TV. I think Ethel is in the kitchen."

"Did you want to see if Cyn and Meg wanted to come?'

"I did. They said next time. They were in the middle of Dirty Dancing and said they weren't moving till the end."

We walked out the front door, straight into Troy's truck that he had idling smack dab in front of the front door.

"Door to door service, ladies," Troy smirked as Marley climbed in, placing a kiss on Troy's cheek.

"Well, aren't you just a gentleman." I hoisted myself up into the jacked up truck and slammed the door shut. "Think your truck is high enough?" I asked, buckling my seat belt.

"Women like big hair, men like big trucks." Troy winked at me over Marley's head and laughed.

"I think big hair went out in the eighties," Marley snickered.

"Yeah, well, big trucks sure as hell didn't." Troy pulled out of the parking lot and headed to the diner across town.

By the time we had pulled into the parking lot of the restaurant, my stomach was growling with hunger, and I was ready to eat an elephant.

First on my to-do list was to order the biggest stack of pancakes ever, devour them, and then head to the salon to give into the change I needed so badly. I was feeling restless and had no idea why.

Hopefully, it only had to do with my hair and not about a tall, handsome man who was taking up too much of my time.

''*'*'*'*'*'*'*'*'*'*'*'*'*

Chapter 6

GAMBLER

I hated the way it smelled here. It felt like death was hanging overhead, the stench of lives lost surrounding me.

The grave was overgrown when I had shown up, and I immediately trimmed away the grass and brushed off the loose leaves and debris that always seemed to gather around the headstone.

I hated coming here, but it also was something I had to do. It had been almost a month since I had come here and it was eating me alive that I had waited so long.

My fingertips grazed over the name engraved on the cold stone, tracing the name of one of the first women I had ever loved.

Evelyn Margret Holmes
1984-2009

She was only twenty-five when she had left too soon. I still remember that day like it was yesterday.

"Sorry, I haven't been by in a while, Evie. Things have been crazy at the clubhouse." I paused, expecting an answer, knowing I wouldn't get one. "I talked to mom the other day. She said she came out to see you last week. From the looks of the grass, it must have been a quick stop to see you."

I glanced around, seeing the undertaker's blue truck enter the far gate and slowly pass by. He raised his hand in hello but didn't stop. "I'll have to talk to Bernie and let him know he needs to take better care when he mows. Although the snow will be flying soon."

I ran my finger through my hair, trying to find more to say. "I told you King met someone, right? Well, now Rigid fell in love with Meg's best friend, Cyn. Gravel finally hooked

45

up with Ethel and Gravel's daughter moved back into town. She works at a salon and started dating Meg's other best friend. Somehow her boss got mixed up in all the shit swirling around the club, and now I'm supposed to keep an eye on her. Her name is Gwen. You'd really like her. She's got a style all her own just like you did."

Maybe that was why I was so drawn to Gwen but pushed her away at the same time. She reminded me so much of Evie when she was alive. Evie was always the life of the party, making friends with everyone. She always wore the craziest clothes, but always made them look good. I never thought I would meet someone like Evie again, and then I met Gwen.

The wind picked up, sending a chill with it that made me pull my coat tight around me. It was definitely fall now. The leaves were changing colors and the days were getting shorter. "I hope you're happy wherever you are, Evie. I miss you every day." My words floated away, silence the only response.

I grabbed the shears I always brought with and headed back to my bike, sticking them into my saddlebag. I didn't know the next time I would find time to come out and talk to Evie, but I knew it would be soon. I never could stay away from her for too long.

As I swung my leg over the bike, my phone dinged, a message coming through.

I swiped the screen and brought up the text Troy had just sent me. *At the salon. You might want to get here when you can.*

Why the hell would I need to get to the salon? I had asked Troy to keep an eye on Gwen for me while I went to church and then headed out here. I had already been gone three hours and wouldn't be back for another hour.

Be back in an hour. I'll meet you at the salon. I pocketed my phone, not waiting for a response and cranked up my bike. I glanced one last time at Evie's grave, wishing things could be different but knew things had happened the way they did for a reason.

Evie was meant to be in my life for only a short time, but it was some of the best moments of my life.

I roared out of the cemetery, leaving Evie behind, headed for the woman who was so much like Evie, but not. When I had lost Evie, I had almost died. I had never known a loss like that before and her death had left a gaping hole in my heart. I hoped I never felt that again. I knew the only way to never feel that again was to never love again. I had been doing a pretty damn good job of it these past seven years, but I had a feeling Gwen was going to have something different to say about my heart being closed off. She might be the one person who could make me love again. Hopefully, I would make it out alive this time again. With only knowing Gwen a short time, I knew she could be the one thing to bring me to my knees and make me beg for mercy.

''*'*'*'*'*'*'*'*'*'*'

Chapter 7

"Holy shit, you look hot. I wanna do that. Can I do that?" Marley rambled to Troy.

"Do whatever you want, sunshine. Although you and Gwen might look like twins if you do orange like her."

"I'm down with that. Gwen is a sexy Rosie the Riveter."

I busted out laughing, assuming my attempt to look like Rosie had been accomplished this morning. "I'm gonna run to the bathroom quickly and then we can head out."

"OK. I'm gonna grab the color book and figure out what color I want to go with," Marley mumbled, walking over to the front desk and started digging through the pile of binders I had stacked on the bottom shelf.

I slipped into the bathroom, lightly shutting the door shut behind me and looked in the mirror.

I had done it. I had put peek-a-boo orange in my hair and it looked sick. After Marley had dyed it, she had blown it out and curled it, making the orange strands stand out.

She had put it half up and then folded my bandana, knotting it, on the top of my head, to hold my hair back. The orange popped out against the black of my hair and I freakin' loved it. It was exactly what I needed.

I fluffed my hair, glancing one last time in the mirror and headed back out to Marley and Troy. "Do you think we could swing by the store and pick up some-" I stopped mid-sentence when I saw Gambler standing where Marley and Troy were. When the hell did he get here?

"We can go wherever you want, doll. You're on the back of my bike now." Gambler was leaning against the front desk, his arms crossed over his chest as his eyes roamed up my body.

Thank goodness I had taken the time to get ready today and not just slap on some yoga pants and call it good. "Marley and Troy can take me where I need to go. They were the ones who brought me here."

"I know who brought you here, doll. I've known where you've been all day."

"How the hell have you known that? I haven't seen you all day." I crossed my arms over my chest, annoyance rolling off of me.

"Text." Son of a bitch. Troy had probably been sending Gambler messages all day about what we were doing.

"Hmmph, whatever. So you get to know where I am at all times, but you can disappear for hours without anyone knowing where you are?"

"The people who needed to know knew where I was."

"Apparently I was not one of the ones who needed to know where you were." I have no idea why that bothered me so much, but it did.

"No, doll. I had some things to take care of. That's all you need to know."

"Hardly seems fair."

"Not much in life is fair. You done playing with your hair?"

Playing with my hair? What an ass. What I did with hair was way more than playing. I doubt Gambler could even do a simple braid. I turned hair into works of art. "Is that what you think I do, play with hair?"

Gambler held his hands up, knowing he was treading on delicate ground. "I didn't mean anything by it."

"Yeah, well, my playing with my hair pays the bills and keeps the lights on."

Gambler walked towards me, the tip of his boots touching the tips of my flats. He reached up, grabbing a strand of orange hair and twirled it around his finger. "Orange?"

Gah, why did he have to get so close? I could smell his cologne float around me, distracting me from the fact I was mad at him five seconds ago. "Yes, orange."

"You know you picked my favorite color, doll?"

I did? Oh shit. I had seen the tank on his bike a week ago and noticed how it was a burnt orange that I loved, but I didn't know it was his favorite color. "It's just a color I picked out." Lie, lie, lie, Gwen. I felt my face heat, hoping Gambler wouldn't see through my lie.

"Hmm, I guess I'll give you that one for right now." He leaned down as I looked up and our eyes locked. "My favorite color or not, doll, you look like a smokin' hot fifties pin-up model."

"Rockabilly," I whispered.

"What, doll?"

"The way I dress, it's called Rockabilly." Not a lot of people knew what that was, especially people in Rockton. When I had moved here to live by my aunt, I had shocked the town. I loved the era of the fifties and the way I dressed reflected that. I wasn't a true rockabilly because I just couldn't get into the music from the forties and fifties. I liked it, but I tended to lean more toward more modern music.

"Well, whatever the fuck it's called, I like it. Especially on you."

"Thank you," I whimpered as his arms snaked around me. This was not good. Not good at all. Being wrapped up in

Gambler's arms made me forget my own name, let alone the fact this man drove me crazy with every word that came out of his mouth.

He stroked my back and I relaxed into his arms and held onto his biceps. "You hungry, doll?"

Hungry? Was I hungry? I had no freakin' clue. All I knew was I wanted to feel Gambler's lips on mine again. "Um, I don't know."

"You don't know if you're hungry?" Gambler smirked.

Sweet Jesus, I needed to pull it together. I had been in the arms of men before and able to keep it together. What the hell was it about Gambler that made me lose it? "Yes, I'm hungry," I said, clearing my throat and tried to step back from Gambler.

His arms tightened around me and he pulled me closer. "Not so fast, doll." He leaned down, his lips a breath away.

"What are we doing, Gambler?"

"Right now?"

I nodded my head yes, unable to form another sentence.

His eyes searched my face and I saw something change. "Nothing, we're doing nothing." Gambler pulled away and turned his back to me. He hung his head down and ran his fingers through his hair.

I stumbled backward, not expecting the change in him. I brushed my fingertips against my lips, wishing he would have let go and kissed me.

This was for the best. Getting tangled up with Gambler was a dead end street that was only going to end up in heartache.

"I'll just grab my purse and then we can go get something to eat," I mumbled, walking into the small back room, not waiting for Gambler to answer.

I grabbed my purse and leaned against the small counter, tilting my head back. What the hell was I doing? Was I really wishing for Gambler to kiss me?

The last time I had given in to what my body had wanted had started out fantastic but then crashed and burned. I couldn't go through what I had gone through before. I had told myself after Matt that I would never fall for another man who would just break my heart.

I couldn't let Gambler in. I was still broken from the last time.

''*'*'*'*'*'*'*'*'*'*

Chapter 8

GAMBLER

Son of a bitch.

God dammit that woman got under my skin in a second and made me forget everything I had been telling myself.

As soon as I had seen her all I wanted to do was pin her to the wall and take everything she had to offer. Her soft, warm body in my arms almost tipped me over the edge.

She mumbled something about grabbing her purse, but I couldn't even turn around to look at her. I needed to get control. I didn't want to need Gwen the way I did. I didn't want the attraction that made me search her out in a crowded room. I just wanted my life to go back to the way it was before Gwen had barged in and started throwing her sass all over and making my body beg for her.

I'd take her to get something to eat and then head back to the clubhouse where there was always someone around and it would keep me from putting my hands on her.

"I'm ready," she chirped from behind me, apparently not as affected as I was.

I rubbed my hands down my face and tried to pull my head out of my ass and get it together. "Where do you feel like eating?" I asked, turning around to look at her. She really did look like a fifties pin-up goddess.

"Why don't we get pizza and take it back to the clubhouse. I'm sure everyone else is hungry."

"Sounds like a plan, doll, but we're going to have to get it delivered. I don't think we can carry ten pizzas on my bike," I laughed.

"Oh, that's right. Well, then we might as well head back to the clubhouse and then we can see what everyone wants." She walked towards the front door, making sure everything was turned off and stood by the front door waiting for me. "You coming?" she asked, cocking her head to the side, smiling at me.

I shook my head, trying to get the image of her swinging hips as she walked to the front door out of my head and grabbed my keys out of my pocket as I walked by her. I slipped out the door, waiting for her to shut and lock it and then walked over to my bike.

"Ever been on a motorcycle?" I grabbed the helmet I had in the saddlebag and handed it to her.

"This is going to give me helmet hair," she complained, handing it back to me.

"I don't give a shit about the fact it's going to wreck your hair. All I care about is that it's going to protect your head in case we crash." I grabbed it from her and set it on her head, snapping the strap shut.

"You don't have to be such a dick," she sassed at me as she adjusted the helmet, trying to fix her hair.

"I'm keeping you safe. If that means I'm a dick, I'm okay with that." I swung my leg over the motorcycle and waited for her to climb on.

"Um," she said, tapping me on the shoulder, "I haven't been on a motorcycle in a long time."

"Swing your leg over and hold on," I smirked, looking over my shoulder at her.

"I'm sure there's more to it than that. If we crash, it's your fault, not mine. I told you it's been awhile." She swung her leg over, kicking me in the side and finally sat down behind me.

"Next time try it without kicking me," I laughed, cranking up the bike.

"You know what, I can totally call Marley to come and pick me up." Gwen sat back from me. I looked over my shoulder and saw her with her arms crossed over her chest glaring at me.

"You're my responsibility, doll. Not Troy's. Where I go, you go. End of story." I yelled over the roar of the engine. I reached back, grabbing her arms and wrapped them around my waist. "Hold on!" I grabbed the handlebars and pulled onto the street. Gwen's arms tightened around me, and I knew she wasn't going to let go until the bike stopped, no matter how pissed off at me she was.

"You're still a dick," she yelled in my ear. I gunned the throttle making Gwen yelp in surprise and wrap her arms around me even tighter.

Good, maybe if she thought I was a dick she would swing those hips at someone else and I could go back to the way things were before I walked into her salon and she tipped my world on its side.

''*'*'*'*'*'*'*'*'*

Gwen

Hold on. Jesus Christ. I was holding on alright. I had the strangest feeling that I was seconds away from death and having the best time of my life. I glanced down, the pavement speeding past underneath us, the white line a blur.

I had never been on a motorcycle before, but not for a lack of trying. I begged my aunt for two years to get a motorcycle when I was sixteen, but she had solidly refused.

She told me when I was eighteen I could get a motorcycle with my own money. Well, eighteen hit and as much as I wanted a bike, the money was never there to get one. Plus, living in Illinois meant I would still have to buy a car for the winter months, so it just made sense to only have a car since I couldn't afford both. Holding on for my life was either curing the need for a motorcycle or feeding the urge. The jury was still out.

Gambler drove like the bike was an extension of his body. He maneuvered the curves with ease, rolling to stops and then rocketing off. We were only five minutes away from the clubhouse, but Gambler took the long way, basically driving to the other side of town and then to the clubhouse.

"Um, I think there might be a quicker way to get to the clubhouse than the one you just took," I said, clambering off the bike and unsnapping the helmet. I took it off, shoving it into Gambler's hands.

"Eh, felt like going for a ride, doll." He shrugged, hanging the helmet from the handlebars.

"No, you wanted to see how many times you could make me shriek."

Gambler leaned in, his lips inches away from mine. "I admit nothing, doll. Just felt like going for a ride."

"You're a dick," I spat back.

"So you keep saying, but I doubt you have anything to back that up."

"Dick."

"Doll."

"I hate you." Ugh, this man was turning me into a pissed off five-year-old.

"No, you don't. You just hate the fact that I was right and I was only trying to keep you safe. You're on the back of my bike, you wear a helmet. King, Rigid, and Gravel have the same rule for when their ol' ladies are on the back of their bikes."

"I'm not you're ol' lady. Ever."

"I never said you were."

"Ahh, I fucking hate you!" I stomped off, pissed that Gambler could evoke such a strong response out of me. I could barely remember the reason I was so pissed at him. I ripped open the door to the clubhouse and walked over to the couch where Cyn and Meg were sitting.

"Love the hair!" Meg gushed, pulling me out of my pissed off mood.

"Thanks, I needed a change." I fluffed my hair, running my fingers through it.

"Told you it was killer," Marley said, walking out of the kitchen.

"Thanks for leaving me with dickhead, Marley." I crossed my arms over my chest.

"Hey," Marley held her hands up, "I tried to stay, but Troy told me we had to go. Plus, it's Gambler. Not like I left you with the some stranger."

"No, not a stranger, but definitely a dick."

"Look, I'm sorry. I figured things were cool between you two since I found you in his bed this morning." Marley plopped down in the recliner and popped open the footrest.

"What? What the hell did I miss?" Cyn asked, looking between Marley and me.

"Shit, I totally forgot to tell you guys. I caught Gwen and Gambler in bed this morning."

"Damn girl, you work fast. Not as fast as Marley though," Meg laughed.

"Bitch," Marley yelled, throwing a pillow at Meg.

"First and last one-night stand, right, sunshine?" Troy bragged, walking out of the kitchen, his mouth full.

"Damn straight," Marley laughed. Troy fell into the recliner next to Marley, tossing his arm around her.

"Look, I need help. Meg, do you think that you could talk to King and try to see if there is someone else who can watch me until this, this... whatever the hell is going on is over." I waved my arms around, not knowing what the hell to call what all this going on was. I knew the bare facts; that the Assassins were after the Knights for some bullshit reason and now everyone was in danger until they figured out what the hell to do.

"I can ask, but I don't think it's going to help. Lo likes to keep club business away from me. Although the club business tried to blow up my house last night, so maybe he might listen to me."

"Please, Meg. You can make that man do anything you want. Flash him some boob and he'll be putty in your hands. I'm begging you. If I have to spend any more time with Gambler, I will not be held responsible for my actions."

"All right. I'll see what I can do tonight. You'll have to deal with him till I talk to Lo."

I glanced over my shoulder at Gambler, who had just walked in the front door. God dammit, why the hell did the man have to look so good? His jeans were molded to his legs and his t-shirt was just tight enough to remind me what he looked like shirtless that it made me want to walk over and rip it off. This man was fucking with my head and it was driving me crazy.

One more day. I could totally handle being around him for one more day without throwing myself at him.

He crooked his finger for me to come over and I rolled my eyes. What the hell did the man want now?

"What?" I asked, walking over to him.

He reached into his back pocket and grabbed his wallet. "Find out what everyone wants and order pizza." I glanced down as he opened his wallet and my eyes bugged out at the wad of cash he thumbed through. He handed me five twenties and shoved his wallet back in his pocket.

"I need one hundred dollars for pizza?" I asked, shocked, grabbing the money.

"You need more, come find me before the guy gets here and let me know."

"Um, I don't think I'll need any more money." I folded the money up and put it in my pocket. "Can't I just order a bunch of different pizzas and just let them go at it?"

"Whatever you want, doll. Just make sure you get one with everything on it and make sure I get a piece." Gambler winked at me and headed down the hall to the bedrooms.

"Did I hear pizza?" Marley asked, walking up to me.

"Um, yeah," I mumbled watching Gambler's retreating back.

"Yes!" Marley pumped her fist in the air. "You want me to order? I'm tight with the owner." Marley pulled her phone out of her pocket and started pushing buttons.

"How the hell are you tight with the pizza guy?"

"I order like three times a week." Marley held her finger up, silencing me. "Mike! It's Marley! How are you?"

Marley walked away talking to whoever the hell Mike was like they were best friends.

I looked around seeing people milling around, most of them I knew, but there were a couple that I had never seen before. I glanced at the clock on the wall seeing it was almost five and wondered where the day went. There was a guy behind the bar handing out drinks and I decided a drink was just exactly what I needed.

Gambler had told me to make myself at home and if I were at home, I would definitely be getting the bottle of vodka out of the cabinet tonight.

"What'll it be, darlin'?" the guy behind the bar asked.

"Gin and tonic. Make it a double." He moved behind the bar grabbing the bottles he needed and started making my drink. "So, what's your name?"

"Demon. I'm the V.P."

I was taken back by the fact that the vice president of the club was making me a drink. I really didn't know a lot about MC's, but I kind of figured the vice president making you a drink was not the norm. "You often sling drinks for the club?"

"Ha. No, not really. It's Turtle's night to be behind the bar, but he's over in the shop finishing up an El Camino, and I told him I would cover for him until he finishes up." He set my drink down in front of me and I took a sip. Pure heaven.

"Well, if it's any consolation, the next time I see you behind the bar I'm going to have you make me five drinks because that is the best gin and tonic I have ever had."

"Gotcha. If all else fails, I can be a bartender." Demon winked at me, his eyes sparkling with humor.

Demon walked away, taking drink orders from other club members, each of them ribbing him about being behind the bar.

I turned around, leaning against the bar, propping my elbows up. Marley and Troy were toe to toe, wrapped in each other's arms. They both had their heads thrown back laughing. I was happy for Marley. She deserved to find her happy ending. Lord knew she had gone through enough to finally find Troy.

My phone buzzed, letting me know I had a text message and pulled it out of my pocket. I turned back to the bar, setting my drink down and opened the message.

I put my two-week notice in today.

Yes! It was about time Paige got up here. Paige was my older sister who still lived in Rhyton. I had been pestering her for the past year that she needed to move to Rockton.

Hell yes! When will you be here? You're moving in with me, right?

LOL. We'll see. I'm not sure I can live with your neat freakiness. We barely made it through childhood without killing each other.

I hated to admit it, but Paige was right. It really was a miracle we had lived to see adulthood. While I was a neat freak and wanted everything in its place, Paige was the complete opposite and seemed to thrive in messy chaos.

OK. If anything, I'll help you find a place to live.

"What put that smile on your face, doll?"

I whirled around, scared by Gambler sneaking up on me. "Jesus, you scared the bejeebus out of me."

Gambler smirked at me and signaled to Demon. Demon grabbed a bottle of whiskey and poured it into a glass full of ice and set it in front of Gambler.

"Sorry, doll. Didn't mean to scare you." He took a sip of his drink and set it down next to mine. "What's got you smiling at your phone like a loon?"

"Oh, um, just my sister. I think she might actually be moving up here in a couple of weeks."

"No shit?" I nodded my head yes and grabbed my drink. "She gonna live with you?"

"Um, I'm trying to convince her to move in with me, but she says we'd clash. She does have a point. Growing up, it's amazing we didn't kill each other." I took a sip of my drink and swirled the liquid in the glass around.

"What made her decide to finally move here?"

"I've been trying to convince her to move here since I did. Ever since our aunt got sick, I've been slowly wearing her down. She put her two-week notice in at work today, so now it's official." I knew I was smiling like a crazy person, but I was so damn excited that Paige was moving here.

"I'm happy for you, doll." He took a sip of his drink and looked me up and down. "You order that pizza?"

"Um," I glanced over his shoulder and saw Marley walking back into the main room. "Marley said she was going to order it. Something about being tight with the owner. Although I really doubt it's going to cost as much as you gave me." I dug into my pocket and handed the money back to him.

He shook his head and drained his glass empty. "Wanna bet?"

"What? No. Just take the money back. You can pay the guy." He set his glass on the bar, signaling to Demon he needed a refill and grabbed the money out of my hand. "Let's make a bet, doll. They don't call me Gambler for nothing." He grabbed a stool, pulling it out for me and motioned for me to sit down.

I hoisted myself up on the stool and set my drink on the bar. "All right, what kind of bet? What happens when I win?"

"Ha. You mean *if* you win. I bet you that the pizza will be more than what I gave you."

"I'll take that bet because I know you are wrong. Now, I repeat, what do I get when I win?"

"You pick, doll. Just like I'll pick what I want when I win."

"Huh," I folded my arms over my chest and rolled my eyes at him. "Well, I wouldn't waste too much time thinking about what you want because you are so going to lose."

"We'll see, doll." Held his hand out for me to shake, a smirk playing on his lips.

I grabbed his hand, shaking it firmly and couldn't wait to see his face when he lost. There was no way this was a bet he was going to win. "You do this often? Make poor bets?"

"You'll see. I never make a bet I know I can't win." He released my hand and grabbed the drink Demon had refilled.

"Oh shit. I know that look. You just made a bet with him, didn't you?" Demon asked, leaning against the bar.

"Hell yeah, I did. Plus, it's a bet he's going to lose. I better think of what I want." I propped my head up on my arm I had rested on the bar.

"You're gonna learn real quick, darlin', that Gambler is not a person you want to make a bet against unless you know for a fact you'll win. He's brutal with what he wants when he wins," Demon warned, shaking his head.

"I'm sure I'll be okay. He handed me over one hundred dollars for pizza and told me I'll probably need more."

Demon just shook his head and walked away. I started doubting my decision when Demon didn't stay to reassure me that I was right. Oh shit.

"Oh my god. Marley told me about your hair, but it looks even more incredible than I pictured." I spun around on my stool and saw Meg and Cyn standing there.

"Oh, you like? It's a bit different, but I like it." I fluffed up my hair, forgetting I had even colored it today.

"It's amazing. Do you think you could put bright purple in mine? Remy told me I was too old to do crazy colors anymore, but I don't care. I'll be the eighty-year-old in the nursing home rocking pink hair and pushing my life alert button to see if any hot firemen show up."

Cyn leaned against the bar and crossed her arms over her chest. "That seems like a pretty accurate guess on what you'll be like."

"I know. I can't wait." Meg rubbed her hands together and laughed like a crazy villain from a cartoon.

"What do you two ladies want to drink?" Demon asked, filling a beer glass for one of the guys.

"Two Old Fashions, extra cherries," Meg called out.

"Sour or sweet?" Demon reached under the bar and grabbed two empty glasses.

"Um, just make it one. And Meg always drinks sweet. I'll have a Sprite or something." Cyn grabbed a barstool behind her and plopped down on it. "I'm so friggin tired, I'm afraid after a drink I'll pass out."

"You're going to make me drink alone, aren't you?" Meg complained.

"Just for tonight. Plus, Gwen is drinking and I'm sure Marley will be, too. You can relive the bathroom incident the last time you drank with her. Just tell Demon to start brewing a pot of coffee." Cyn laughed, grabbing the Sprite Demon set in front of her.

"Um, do I want to know?" I asked.

"You're going to learn real quickly, doll, that when Meg and Cyn are around, craziness is almost guaranteed to ensue. It's best just to stand back and watch." I looked over my shoulder at Gambler, and he threw a wink at me. I turned back to Cyn and Meg and felt him move behind me, putting his arm on the back of my chair.

"Good, sounds like fun." I know Gambler was trying to warn me, but Cyn and Meg look like a hell of a good time that I wanted in on. "Oh, I never got to ask. Are you ok? How bad is your house?"

Meg waved her hand at me and took a drink. "Eh, it's kind of messed up. They tossed it onto the front porch so of course the porch is toast, but thankfully it didn't really hurt the house and we were all safe. I'm more pissed at the fact my favorite chair is now smithereens. It was the perfect chair to sit in, sipping cocktails and watch Lo work on his bike."

"She's going on and on about the damn chair again, isn't she?" King walked up behind Meg and wrapped his arms around her, kissing her on the side of the head.

"Eh, he knows me so well." She shrugged her shoulders and drained half of her glass in one drink.

"Well, thank God you were all OK and I'm sure you can find another chair. It's the perfect reason to go shopping,"

I laughed. I tried to take a sip of my drink but was surprised that all that was left was ice cubes. Gambler grabbed it out of my hand and set it on the bar, shaking his head at me.

"Going down like water, doll."

"It was a long day," I said, shrugging my shoulders at him.

"Pizza will be here in probably ten minutes. Mike said he'll put a rush on it. I told him we had twenty hungry bikers." Marley walked up to our group, a wine cooler dangling from her fingertips.

"How much was it?" I asked.

"One-."

"Eh!" Gambler threw his hand up, silencing Marley. "We'll wait till the guy gets here."

Marley looked at Gambler like he was crazy but didn't finish her sentence. "Ok."

"Is that really all you are going to drink tonight? I just almost got blew up. We need to celebrate. Shots!" Meg yelled, raising her hand in the air. She stood on the ring of her bar stool and leaned over the bar, grabbing the first bottle she touched.

"Hey, hey, hey. My bar, my rules." Demon grabbed the bottle out of her hand, setting it back down.

"Ok, whatever," she said, sitting back down. "We need shots. Buttery Nipples, four of them," Meg ordered.

"I swear to Christ, she doesn't hear a word I say," Cyn mumbled, standing up. "Make it three, Demon. I'm headed back to Rigid's room. I'll be out for some pizza later." Cyn shuffled down the hall, not waiting for a response.

"She ok?" King asked, watching Cyn disappear down the hall.

"She's been a crab ass lately. I think she's coming down with something. She was fine this morning when we were watching movies." Meg's eyes also watched Cyn walk away.

"Maybe someone should check on her," Marley said.

"I'm sure Rigid won't be far behind. He had some shit to finish in the shop. Once he gets his ass in here, we'll let him know about Cyn." Lo pulled his phone out of his pocket, glancing at it and shoved it into his pocket.

"You waiting for an important call?" Meg asked, grabbing the three shots Demon poured and handed them to Marley and me.

"Just checking to make sure I didn't miss any calls, babe."

"OK! Let's toast!" Meg raised her glass. "To the fact that my ass is not a toasty human marshmallow right now." Meg clinked her glass against ours and tossed her shot back. Marley and I followed suit, the shot going down smoothly.

Marley started coughing the instant she drank it and Gambler patted her on the back.

"Yo, pizza is here!" a guy by the door yelled.

"Oh hell yes, time for me to win a bet." I set my drink down and beelined to the door, dodging people and trying to not to spill their drinks. "How much is it?" I asked, pushing the guy who had had opened the door out of the way.

The delivery boy's eyes were bugged out, and he looked at me in shock, "Ugh, that'll be one ninety-nine and fifty-four cents," he mumbled, thrusting the receipt at me.

"What the fuck." I scanned the receipt, counting 15 pizzas were ordered. "Holy shit."

"Why do you look so shocked, doll?" Gambler asked, coming up behind me, resting his hand on my hip.

"Because you were fucking right! Who the hell orders fifteen pizzas?"

"I do. Have you seen how many people are here? I doubt this will even be enough. I plan on devouring half of one by myself." Marley walked up, rubbing her hands together.

"Uh, you think I could get some help carrying these in?" The delivery boy looked around, his eyes huge saucers of awe as he looked at all the bikers.

"Roam, Ham, Turtle. Help bring the pizzas in," King yelled. The three guys filed out the door with Marley following behind, hot on the heels of the delivery guy.

"I do believe this means I won," Gambler said, pulling out the money he had handed me before. He opened his wallet and pulled out an extra twenty.

"It really wasn't a fair bet because I'm sure you've ordered pizza for this many people before. The most I've ever ordered for is four people. The bet is off," I huffed, crossing my arms over my chest. I knew Gambler wasn't going to let it go, but I had to try. I was terrified of what he was going to want for winning.

"Another thing you don't know about me, doll," he leaned in his face an inch away from mine. "I collect on every bet. Every time."

"This wasn't fair."

"Demon tried to warn you, doll. He knows I'm ruthless. I guess you just figured that out, too. I'll let you know what I want when I think of it." He winked at me and walked out the door.

Son of a bitch. I had no idea what Gambler was going to want from me. The possibilities were endless of the things he could want.

"Lost that bet, didn't you darlin'?" Demon asked, walking up to me.

"Hell yes. You could have warned me a little better. I didn't get a danger Will Robinson vibe from you at all. I thought you were just joking. Now I have to wait and see what Gambler is going to want since he won." I crossed my arms over my chest, pouting.

"I wouldn't worry too much about it. Gambler's a good guy most of the time." Demon winked at me, a smirk plastered on his face.

"It's the 'most of the time' I'm worried about." Gambler and guys walked passed us, there arms full of pizza boxes and set them down on the pool table. Marley walked in the door, one pizza box in her hands, the lid open.

"Couldn't wait?" I asked.

"I can never wait for pizza. Roam wanted me to grab a couple. I told him I was only out there for my dinner." She took a bite of a slice, cheese stringing from her face. "So fucking good," she mumbled her mouth full.

I reached into her box to grab a slice, but she slammed the lid shut on my hand. "No touchy." She waved her finger at me and walked away. Jesus, remember not to get between Marley and her pizza.

"Doll, come eat before these fuckers eat it all," Gambler called, a slice raised to his mouth.

Oh, Jesus. Why the hell did he have to look so sexy? Why did he have to make me want things I promised myself I would never want again? Gambler had trouble and heartbreaker written all over him. I needed to remember that.

Gambler was a one-way street to heartbreak. Time to find a detour around him.

But first, I needed a drink.

''*'*'*'*'*'*'*'*'*'*'*'*

Chapter 9

GAMBLER

"I've only had four drinks," Gwen said holding five fingers up in my face.

"That's five, doll."

"No, it's five." All I could do is shake my head and laugh.

After the pizza had come, Gwen had polished off half a pizza all by herself and slammed two gin and tonics in a matter of minutes. Throw in Meg yelling shots every ten minutes, Gwen was hammered.

"Let's get you to bed, doll. I really don't think you want to sleep on a pool table tonight. I had been trying to wrangle Gwen down the hall to my room, but she had veered over to the pool table and was now sprawled out on top of it. People had slept on the pool table before, but never in the middle of Roam and Demon's game.

"I think I can get it around her arm if she doesn't move," Roam said, closing one eye, squinting, and lined up his shot.

"Son of a bitch," I grabbed Gwen off the table seconds before Roam's pool stick connected with the ball. I tossed her over my shoulder and headed down the hall.

"Wait, wait, I didn't say byeeee to Meg. Or Marley." She pounded on my back, trying to make me stop.

I detoured over to Meg and Marley, who were sitting on top of the bar and swung Gwen around to see them.

"Gambler says I have to go to bed. He's a pooper. A party. I mean, aw fuck. I don't know," she rattled on, not able to put two sentences together.

"King is trying to get me into bed, too." Meg reached out, petting Gwen's head. "He's bossy but sooo hot. Like a taco, hot."

Marley burst out laughing, tossing her head back, falling off the bar. Thankfully Turtle was walking by and he broke her fall. "Oh no, I broke the turtle," Marley laughed, shakily getting up off the floor.

"I think it's everyone's time for bed," Troy said, walking around the bar, helping Turtle off the floor.

"What the hell just happened?" he asked, watching Marley lean heavily against the bar.

"I think we should have cut them off two drinks ago." Troy patted Turtle on the back and walked over to Marley to help steady her.

"OK, doll, time for bed." I nodded at Troy and King, knowing they were going to have as much fun as I was about to have hauling Gwen to bed.

"Bye, Ladies! You all kick ass!" Gwen called as we walked down the hall. We turned the corner to my room, and she fell silent.

"You ok, doll?"

She patted my leg but didn't say anything.

I grabbed my keys out of my pocket and opened the door, pushing it open with my foot. I flipped the light switch on and saw Mr. T sitting in the middle of the bed, waiting for us.

72

I slid Gwen down till her feet touched the floor, but I didn't let go of her. "Why were you so nice tonight," she mumbled into my neck.

"Did you want me to be an ass, doll?"

"Hmm, most guys would have."

"I'm not most guys. You had fun, nothing to get mad at." She leaned back, her hair all over the place, covering her face. I brushed it aside, her eyes closed, and she hummed under her breath.

"You're smooookin' hot. Tall, hot, and nice. Stop it." She reached up and punched me in the shoulder.

"You said hot twice," I laughed.

"That's because it needs to be said twice. Better make it three. You're hot." She ran her fingers through her hair, cascading it all around her face again and tried blowing the piece that had fallen in her face out of the way.

"You're hot, too, doll." I brushed her hair out of her face again, and she smiled up at me. "Let's get you ready for bed. You wanna use the bathroom first?" It would have been the perfect time to kiss Gwen again, but I knew she was totally tanked, and I didn't want to take advantage of her.

"Pee, then cuddles." She pushed out of my arms and stumbled to the bathroom, thankfully making it without falling.

Cuddles? Gwen must *really* be drunk. Most of the times it felt like she was seconds away from scratching my eyes out.

"Gambler?" My head whipped to the door, and I listened closely. "Gambler?" I heard her quietly mumble.

"You need me, doll?"

"I shouldn't want you, but I do."

What the hell? Drunk Gwen was confusing as fuck. "So you want me to come in or you're good?"

"Come in, I need help," she whined. I heard a thump against the wall, and I bolted to the door, throwing it open.

Gwen was slumped over on the floor, her cheek pressed against the cold tile of the floor. I knelt down next to her and gently shook her shoulder. Her eyes fluttered open and she moaned. "Tell me what you need, doll."

"To go back five hours and not drink so much," she complained, shutting her eyes again.

"I can't help you with that, but I can help you get undressed and into bed. I'll get you some water and Tylenol too."

"Hmm, let's just stay here. I'm hot."

"Not happening. You'll end up with a sore neck and smelling like pine sol in the morning. Come on, babe." I gently helped her sit up and rested her against the wall. "You ok there for a second?" I asked, standing up and looked down at her.

"Oh yeah. Totally good," she said, holding her fingers up in a peace sign. I laughed because honestly, this was one of the funniest things I had seen in a while. I opened the medicine cabinet, glancing over my shoulder making sure Gwen hadn't slumped over again and grabbed the bottle of Tylenol down and filled a glass with water. "Be right back," I mumbled as I stepped out the door and set the pills and water next to the bed.

"Gambler," she called, panic in her voice

"I'm coming, doll."

"Oh, I thought you left," she mumbled, closing her eyes again.

"I told ya I was going in the other room, doll. Did you fall asleep for fifteen seconds?" I laughed, bending down, gathering her in my arms and lifted her up.

"Whoa, who knew you were hot and strong," she whispered, resting her head on my shoulder.

"You weigh nothing, doll. I'm pretty sure I could pick two of you up."

"Hardly, my butt is big and I got pudge."

"Pudge?" I asked, not knowing what the hell she was talking about. I set her down on the bed, and she fell back, sprawling out on the bed.

She lifted her shirt up and pointed at her stomach. "This, is pudge." She put her hand on her stomach and giggled it. "Jiggly pudge," she laughed.

"You're crazy. Give me a foot." She held her leg up, and I quickly slid off her shoe and repeated the same with the other foot. "We need to get you out of these clothes. You OK with me undressing you?"

"Whatever, it's not like it's something you haven't seen before," she said, waving her hand around.

I just shook my head, not wanting to get into a fight with Gwen when she was drunk. "Sit up for one second, doll." She held her hands up for me to grab, but didn't make any moves. I grabbed her arms that were limp like wet spaghetti and pulled her up. "Hold on to my neck," I ordered, lacing her fingers behind my neck.

She held on as I pulled the hem of her t-shirt up and lifted her arms from my neck as I pulled the shirt up. I tossed her shirt behind my back and pushed her back to lay down. I tried my hardest not to focus on her pale orange bra that pushed her breasts up, putting them on display. I popped the button of her jeans and slid the zipper down. Fuck me. Matching panties. I gritted my teeth and tried to focus on the task at hand. Get Gwen undressed and in bed.

"Who would have thought I'd be letting you into my pants this soon," she giggled, smothering her mouth with her hand. Her eyes danced with laughter, and I had never seen a more beautiful woman in my life. Wasn't it some shit that she was too far gone to even know what she was saying and doing right now.

She propped herself up on her elbows and watched as I slid her pants down her legs and over her feet. I threw them in the same direction as her shirt and pulled back the covers of the bed. "Slide in," I ordered, holding my hand out to her.

She grabbed my hand and shimmied up to the top of the bed, and I pulled the covers over her. "You need to take some Tylenol, doll. It'll help with the headache you're probably going to have in the morning.

She sat up and took the three pills I shook out of the bottle and shakily grabbed the glass of water. She popped the pills into her mouth and drained the glass of water. After she had handed it back to me, she wiped her mouth with the back of her hand and fell back into the mound of pillows.

I set the glass of water back down and headed back into the bathroom.

"Do you like me, Gambler?" Gwen called.

Shit, I thought for sure she was going to pass out again. I bent over and unlaced my boots and tried to figure out what to say. "Um, of course, I do." I did, I just didn't need her to know *how* much I liked her. I had been fighting my attraction to her all night. Every time she would laugh, she would run her fingers through her hair, cascading it all down her back making my fingers itch wanting to feel how soft her hair was.

"I wish you had some food in here, I'm starving." I was coming to find out that when Gwen was drunk, she was very random. I pulled my shirt over my head and kicked off my boots next to the shower.

"I can run and get you something from the kitchen if you're hungry," I called, running the water in the sink and splashed my face.

"There he goes being nice again," she mumbled. "Do you think there's ice cream?"

"I'm sure there is. Ever since Meg and Cyn have been hanging around, there's always food. I'm sure one of them bought ice cream." Gwen didn't answer, but I left my pants on figuring I was going to head to the kitchen. I grabbed my toothbrush, squirting toothpaste on it and gave my teeth a quick brush. I looked in the mirror and wondered what the hell I was doing. Didn't I say to myself this morning that I couldn't be with Gwen, and now I had her in my bed and was going to get her ice cream because she was craving it?

This woman was getting under my skin, and I had no idea how to stop it. All night I had stayed close to her, not wanting to leave her side. Her laugh was contagious and she had the brothers eating out of her hand with her crazy stories from the salon and her smile that lit up the room.

I flipped the light off, not having a clue about what I was going to do about Gwen. The damn woman made me happy and I couldn't tell you the last time that had happened. "You want me to get ice cream?" I asked, but Gwen didn't answer.

Her eyes were closed, and she was lightly snoring. Her mouth was hanging open, and she had never looked more adorable. Her hair was fanned out on the pillow and the blanket was pulled down to her waist.

She was right when she had said that her being undressed was something I hadn't seen before, but with Gwen it was different. She wasn't some woman in my bed for a couple hours of fun and then be on her way, probably never to be seen again. Gwen made me feel things I never thought I could feel about someone.

When Evie had died, a part of me died with her. She was my only sister and was amazing. There were still days I would forget she was gone and I'd get the urge to call her. She wasn't supposed to be taken away that soon. She was only twenty-five. She had her whole life in front of her when a semi had plowed into her on that icy morning. She was a bakery manager and she always worked early mornings. She was always out on the road it seemed before the plows could get out there.

She was driving on the highway, probably listening to that shitty pop music she always made me listen to when her life was over in a second. When I had gotten the call, I lost it. King had to drive me to the accident and hold me back when I saw her.

Her beautiful, bright, smiling face was pale and bloodied with pieces of glass scattered around her. Gwen's smile and laughter reminded me so much of Evie. Maybe that was why I needed to be around her. She brought back a part of me that I had thought died.

Gwen rolled over, turning her back to me and hugged my pillow to her. Mr. T hopped up on the bed and burrowed under the covers with his human.

Enough standing over Gwen, watching her like a stalker. I took my jeans off, throwing them over the back of the chair and turned the light off. Just as I was about to slide under the covers, I remember that Gwen needs the light on. I padded over to the bathroom, flipped the light on and shut the door, leaving a sliver of light shining into the room.

As I slid under the covers, she curled into me, her head resting on my shoulder and she hummed quietly under her breath. She settled, resting her hand on my chest, and I breathed a sigh of relief when she didn't wake up.

I shut my eyes, willing myself to fall asleep. It didn't work. All I could think about was Gwen's warm, soft body pressed against mine and how much I wanted to make her mine and never let anything happen to her.

I was falling for her and there was nothing I could do to stop it.

''*'*'*'*'*'*'*'*'*'*'*

Chapter 10

Gwen

I cracked on eye open and it felt like the whole world was spinning around me. What the hell had I done last night? I thought back, trying to remember, and all I could remember was Meg yelling shots all the time.

Oh Lord, shots had done this to me. I closed my eye, hoping that would make the world stop tilting back and forth. I moved my arm and felt my pillow move underneath me. I froze, realizing I wasn't in bed by myself.

"How bad do you feel?" Gambler rumbled.

"Like death," I croaked.

"I guess you'll have that after drinking a bottle of Southern Comfort between the three of you. I'm sure Meg and Marley are feeling the same this morning."

"I blame Meg," I groaned.

Gambler laughed and rolled towards me, his arm staying under my head. God dammit, this man even looked good right away in the morning. His hair was ruffled and sticking up, but his gorgeous eyes were shining brightly at me, a grin spread across his lips. "You want me to run and get you coffee?"

I blinked, surprised. Did he just offer to get me coffee? The almighty beverage of the Gods. "Hell yes, three."

Gambler chuckled, his arm wrapping around my neck and he pulled me close. "How about you start with one and we'll see how your stomach handles that." He threw the covers back and rolled out of bed.

I glanced down and saw I was only in my bra and panties. How the hell did that happen? "Holy shit." I grabbed the covers and pulled them up to my chin. "Where the hell are my clothes?"

"Somewhere on the floor. I was more concerned with getting you into bed, not where your clothes fell.

"We didn't," I pointed between Gambler and myself, terrified I had made a terrible decision last night.

Gambler grabbed a black t-shirt out of the dresser and pulled it over his head. "No, doll. All you did was talk, a lot. Scouts honor."

"I really doubt that you were a cub scout," I scoffed.

"I plead the fifth," he turned around and winked at me. "I'll be back with your coffee. You should probably take some more Tylenol, doll, it'll help with that freight train that is running through your head right now." Gambler walked out the door, closing it tight behind him.

OK, so we didn't have sex. I think. But what the hell did happen last night? I remember having a hell of a time with Marley and Meg and the never ending bottle of Southern Comfort, but that's it.

At one-point Meg and Marley had tried to do chicken fights on King and Troy's shoulders, but both had ended up on the floor laughing their asses off when they couldn't even get on the guy's shoulders. Gambler had stayed close to my side the whole night, attentive and quiet. I figured he was staying close so I didn't embarrass myself or him. I'm sure Marley, Meg, and I were quite a sight last night.

Now, I needed to remember how the hell my clothes came off. Mr. T hopped up on the bed, stretching as he walked, his tail wagging rythmacially. "Hello, pretty man," I cooed as he bumped my hand I held out to him, rubbing against it. "Did you see how my clothes came off, pretty man?" T just purred as I rubbed his neck, ignoring my question.

"I didn't know how you like it. I drink mine black, so I just made yours that way, too." Gambler walked through the door, holding both cups in front of him.

"Black's good."

He walked over to the side of the bed and held my cup out to me. "Thank god you don't drink it with all that sissy shit like Meg and Cyn do. I swear there are fifty different kinds of creamer in the fridge." Gambler curled his lip in disgust and took a sip of coffee. He stared down at me, his eyes scanning me. "You still trying to figure out how your clothes came off?" He smirked.

"I'm hoping I was the one who took them off, but from what I remember, it would have been amazing if I had."

"You gonna drink that coffee, or wait till it turns cold?"

I had stuck one arm out from the blanket to grab the coffee but was afraid the blanket would fall if I made one wrong move. I know Gambler had seen me last night, but now it was different. I was sober and would remember everything. "Um, of course." I hesitantly raised my arm, and leaned forward, my chin pressed down on the blanket, praying it wouldn't fall.

"That's an interesting way to drink coffee," he laughed, walking toward the bathroom. He shut the door behind him, and I breathed a sigh of relief. I set my coffee on the bedside table and tossed the covers back and jumped from the bed. I grabbed my suitcase from under the bed and tossed it open, frantically trying to get dressed before Gambler came out of the bathroom.

I grabbed my favorite faded Def Leppard shirt and a pair of black leggings. I pulled them on quickly, thankful the shirt was baggy and covered my ass. I grabbed a hair tie, finger combing my hair and pulled it back. "I see you found some clothes."

I whirled around at Gambler's words, my arms over my head, tightening my ponytail. "Um, yeah. I plan to remember how these come off, too."

"Then I would stay away from Meg and her bottle of Southern Comfort."

"Truer words have never been spoken," I moaned as I lowered my arms.

"You got any plans today?"

"None that I know of. I normally do laundry and read on my days off."

"Well, Meg and Cyn got this crazy fucking idea that they need to go to the pumpkin patch today and wanted me to ask you if you wanted to come with."

"Are you going to come?" I wanted him to come, but I didn't.

"I think we were all going to ride out there on our bikes. Make the day of it before Meg and Cyn need to go to work."

"Isn't it too cold?"

"Just make sure you put on a coat and you'll be fine, doll. Riding in the fall is one of the best times to go." Gambler walked over to the end of the bed where he had kicked his boots off and picked them up and grabbed a pair of socks out of his dresser. "You'll be behind me so the wind shouldn't be too bad."

"OK, I guess that sounds like fun. Are Marley and Troy coming along?" I grabbed a pair of socks out of my bag and pulled my other suitcase out from under the bed that had all my shoes in it. Thankfully I had packed a black pair of boots and had second thoughts on my decision to wear leggings. "I'm gonna change my pants," I mumbled, walking back over to my other suitcase and pulled out a pair of jeans.

"Whatever you say, doll. I'm gonna grab another cup of coffee before we take off. You want anything to eat?" He stood up, his boots already laced.

I needed to hurry the hell up. "Um, just some toast or something."

Gambler nodded his head at me and walked out the door. I pulled off my leggings, tossing them towards my open suitcase and pulled my jeans on. I traded my t-shirt for a long sleeve Henley I had packed. I took my hair down from the messy ponytail I had thrown it up and walked into the bathroom.

"Holy fuck," I moaned when I looked in the mirror. I couldn't believe that I was actually going to leave the room looking like this. I grabbed my makeup bag off the tank of the toilet and rummaged through it looking for all the necessary tools to make me look presentable.

I wiped off the makeup that was still smudged all over my face and started fresh. I forgoed foundation and moved on to the heavy bags under my eyes. I smeared on concealer praying the make-up gods were on my side and topped it off with powder.

By the time I was done, I had been in the bathroom for twenty minutes and looked like I was ready to join the human world again. I grabbed my jean jacket out of my bag, shaking it out, and threw it on.

I scratched Mr. T behind his ears, checked to make sure his food bowl was full and jetted out the door, down the hall to the main room.

"It's about time you got your ass out here," Meg called as she walked out of the kitchen.

"I woke up looking like ass. It's a miracle how I look now."

"I doubt you could ever look like ass. Come on. Gambler said you needed to eat, but we all decided to stop at the diner on the way out of town and eat there." Meg threaded her arm through mine and we walked over to the group that was gathered around the bar.

"Bout time you came out, doll." Gambler walked over to me, his eyes scanning me up and down. "Although, it was worth every second," he mumbled. I blushed under his gaze and clasped my hands in front of me.

"Um, thanks," I mumbled, unsure of what else to say.

"All right, let's hit it. Meg and Cyn need to be back by three to get to work," King called and headed to the door, Meg tucked under his arm. I didn't have a chance to ask her if she was hung over, but it didn't appear that she was. How the hell did she manage that?

"Are Marley and Troy coming with us?" I asked, glancing around trying to get a glimpse of them.

"Marley isn't used to how people from Wisconsin drink. She's nursing one hell of a hangover right now. Her and Troy are staying behind," Cyn laughed as she walked past, hand in hand with Rigid.

"Oh, that sucks. Although it is true. I don't know how ya'll drink so much and still function as a human being the next day." Gambler grabbed my hand and led me out the door following Cyn and Rigid.

"That's how we keep warm on cold nights. Well, that and something else," Rigid laughed, handing a helmet to Cyn. She strapped it on, and I looked over to Meg, who was doing the same thing. Gambler gave me the helmet he always made me wear and I looked at King and Rigid.

"How come ya'll don't wear helmets?" I asked as I strapped it on.

"I've never worn one. Stupid, I know. I think King and Rigid are the same. The reason you ladies need to wear one is because we need to keep ya'll safe." Gambler threw his leg over the bike and climbed on.

"You know how stupid that sounds when you say that, right?" I slid on behind him and wrapped my arms around his middle and held on.

"You'll get used to it," Cyn called. "I've been arguing with Rigid for months to wear one, but he refuses. I'll wear him down one day."

All the men fire up their bikes, Gambler's bike coming to life under me, and we all headed to the edge of town where the diner was.

I was again amazed at how well Gambler handled the bike, driving it with ease and practice. When we pulled up to the restaurant, my stomach growled in protest just as Gambler killed the bike. His body shook undermine, his laughter ringing out.

"You hungry, doll?" Gambler asked.

"Damn near starved," I grumbled, sliding off the bike. "Hey, didn't I ask you to get me ice cream last night?" I asked as I watched Gambler stand up.

"Yeah, and I was almost out the door but you passed out before I could even step foot out the door."

"Oh, well. That would explain why I'm so hungry." I pouted, sticking my lip out.

"Come on, doll, I'll feed ya," Gambler held his hand out to me and I hesitated. It felt like he was asking for a whole lot more than just walking me to the door of the diner. I looked up from his hand, his eyes studying me. This was a test and I didn't want to fail. "Come on, Gwen," he whispered.

I reached out, his fingers threading through mine and tugged me towards the diner. His warm hand gripped mine, and I felt something I hadn't felt in a long time. I trusted him. He held the door open for me. I walked past him, but he stopped me midway.

"You look beautiful today, doll," he whispered, pressing a kiss to the side of my head.

I looked up at him, unable to read his eyes and smiled. "Somethings are worth waiting for, I guess, right?"

"I think you're more than worth waiting for, doll. Just don't make me wait too long." He leaned down, his lips inches away. "I promise to make it worth it." He pressed his lips to mine, the sweetest kiss I had ever felt. That kiss held the promise that there was more to come and I was damn near ready to find out just what kind of promise that was.

''*'*'*'*'*'*'*'*'*'*

Chapter 11

GAMBLER

"Three eggs, scrambled, toast, three sausage links, not the patties, two pancakes, and half a grapefruit." Gwen shut her menu and looked up at the waitress. Her pen was going a mile a minute trying to write down everything Gwen wanted.

"Um, is that?" she asked, her pen poised to write down more.

"Can you add strawberries and whipped cream to the pancakes?"

"Sure thing, hun." The waitress turned her attention to take Cyn's order but my eyes stayed glued to Gwen.

"You hungry, doll?"

"Beyond starved. I'm still pissed you didn't get me ice cream last night. You should have woke my ass up."

I grabbed a straw, stripping off the wrapper and stuck it in my glass of water. "I thought sleeping was more important than ice cream."

"Nothing is more important than ice cream. Ever."

"I'll remember that the next time you are drunk off your ass and demand ice cream."

"You better."

I tossed my arm over the back of the booth, pulling her to me. "What happens if I don't? Although you do have a losing bet you need to honor yet."

She turned her head towards me, a snarl on her lips. "I didn't lose. The bet was off because you lied."

"No way, doll. We shook on it. A bet is a bet." I lowered my voice, not wanting anyone to hear.

"We'll see about that," she whispered back.

"Are we going to bet on the fact of whether or not you fulfill your end of the last bet?" Stubborn as a mule. I was going to cash in her debt. Guaranteed.

"Yes."

"You do know how ridiculous this is," she just shook her head at me, not giving up. "Well, I'm assuming the terms of this bet are, you win, you don't have to fulfill the old bet. If I win, you have to do two things for me."

"Deal, because you are not going to win." She grabbed my hand, shaking it and pulled away from me. "You're going down, Gambler."

I leaned towards her, nose to nose. "Oh, I plan on it, doll, and I'm going to enjoy it just as much as you are." Her jaw dropped at my words and she reared back.

I sat back, smug, knowing that I was going to get Gwen right where I wanted her whether she liked it or not.

''*'*'*'*'*'*'*'*'*'*'*'*'

Gwen

"Oh shit, things are getting interesting over there," Meg called, smirking at me as she emptied two packets of sugar into her coffee.

"Ya'll want coffee?" The waitress asked the pot lifted, waiting.

I looked around seeing everyone else had their cups filled and were staring at Gambler and me, "Black," we said at the same time. Cyn and Meg broke down into a fit of giggles while King and Rigid just shook their heads.

After the waitress had filled our cups, I had to make an escape and get my wits about me. "I'm gonna run to the restroom before the food comes." I bumped Gambler, urging him to get his ass out of my way.

"Running away, doll?" he whispered as he slid out of the booth.

"You wish," I hissed back. I hightailed it to the bathroom, shutting the door behind me. I leaned against the door, resting my head back and screamed when there was a knock on the door. "Someone's in here," I hollered when they knocked again.

"We know, now let us the hell in." Wait, was that Meg? We, who the hell was we?

I turned the handle on the door, and before I could pull it open, it was being pushed into, and I took a step back before I got plowed over.

"Scoot in, woman. This bathroom is tiny," Meg ordered as she shut the door behind her as Cyn and her crowded in.

"Because it's only meant for one person," I said, standing in the corner between the sink and the wall.

"Would you squish over, I'm gonna have to straddle the toilet," Cyn complained.

"Just sit on the damn toilet. That'll give us more room." Meg ordered, lowering the seat and Cyn sat down.

"I can't believe this is happening," I said, running my fingers through my hair. All I wanted to do was go to the bathroom to get away from Gambler for a second, and now I was crowded into a four by four bathroom with Mutt and Jeff.

"Believe it. It's easier that way," Cyn advised, crossing her legs.

"So what's the deal with you and Gambler?" Meg said, crossing her arms over her chest, except she knocked Cyn in the head as she did it.

"Would you watch what the hell you are doing?" Cyn rubbed the side of her head, scowling at Meg.

"You've got a hard head, you'll be fine," Meg said, waving Cyn off. "Now, back to you and Gambler." Her eyes bore into me, almost like she was trying to read my mind.

"Oh Jesus, Meg. Stop trying to read her mind," Cyn said, punching Meg in the leg.

"Hey, you never know if you can read minds unless you try." Meg flipped off Cyn and stuck her tongue out at her.

I was in the twilight zone. I had to be in another dimension, because in my normal life, I never would be trapped in a tiny bathroom with Cyn and Meg. "Um, nothing is going on with Gambler and me," I mumbled, hoping Cyn and Meg would leave.

"I'm not buying it. I saw the way that man was looking at you earlier." Meg tried moving closer but stepped on Cyn's foot.

"For all that is holy, would you stop moving?! There's nowhere to fucking go, Meg!" Cyn cursed, grabbing her foot and rubbed it.

"Sorry, but you know you have snow skis for feet. It was inevitable I would step on them."

"You did not just go there. You have the same size feet as I do!"

"Details," Meg mumbled.

"I swear to god it's a good thing I love you, or I would definitely rethink you being Godmother to my baby." Cyn glared at Meg and put both of her feet on the ground.

"I've got time before that. At least a year."

"More like eight months," Cyn muttered.

"Plenty of time," Meg looked back at me, ready to pounce on the whole Gambler issue. Except, she didn't, because it finally sunk in what Cyn had just said. Holy shit, Cyn was pregnant. That explained her mood swings and weird eating habits lately. Not to mention the wanting to sleep all the time. She had a baby Rigid in the oven.

Meg's jaw dropped open, and she made a weird baaing sound. Not exactly the reaction I expected from her.

"Are you gonna say anything or just act like a sheep until I pop this baby out?"

"You... You have a..." Meg rocked her arms, pretending to hold a baby and pointed at Cyn.

"Jesus Christ, she's resorted to charades now," Cyn said, rolling her eyes.

Meg slapped her hand over her mouth and screamed. "At least, she's making a different noise now," I laughed as Cyn slapped her leg again.

"Knock it off, you didn't act like this the first time I was pregnant." I didn't know all the details, but I knew Cyn had been pregnant by her asshole of an ex before she met Rigid.

"That's because this time you're having a baby with someone you love. I was over the moon excited the last time, too, but now I get to be excited for Rigid, too. Oh, my god, you are going to have the cutest babies!" Meg clapped her hands together and bounced on the balls of her feet. "This is the most fantastic thing ever."

"It does feel different now. Rigid is so careful with me he's driving me insane. He told me today is my last ride on his bike until the baby comes. I swear he's going to wrap me in bubble wrap." Cyn put her hand on her stomach, rubbing it.

"Congratulations," I said, leaning down, wrapping her up in a hug. Cyn's pregnancy was way more exciting than whatever the hell was going on with Gambler and me.

Meg wrapped her arms around Cyn and I and squeezed the hell out us. "I'm gonna be an auntie. I can spoil the shit out of him and then give him back when he's naughty. Win, win."

"Oh Lord, it's already starting," Cyn wheezed out.

"Babe," King called out as he pounded on the door.

"Shit," Meg stepped back and wiped the tears from her eyes. "You made me cry, bitch," she laughed.

"I'm always on the verge of tears lately. Welcome to the club." Cyn stood up, bumping into Meg and I and reached for a paper towel. She wiped her eyes and tossed it in the garbage. "We never did hear about you and Gambler."

I backed up, my back against the wall, and shrunk down under their stares. "Don't look at me like that. I have no freakin' clue."

"Well, do you like him?" Meg asked, crossing her arms over her chest.

"The man drives me insane."

"Do you think he's hot?"

Ugh, that was an understatement. I thought he was the most gorgeous man I had ever seen. "He's OK."

"I think you think he's more than OK. What the hell is the problem?"

"Babe, the food is here. If you want to be back in time for work tonight, we need to eat and get a move on," King said through the door.

Meg stomped her foot and whirled around, and yanked open the door. "We're in the middle of something, Lo."

"Cyn's pregnant. Come freak out at the table," Lo said, grabbing her hand.

Meg sputtered, struggling to get a sentence out. "You... how... tell... You knew and didn't tell me!"

"I found out five minutes ago when I wondered what the hell you three were doing and Rigid said Cyn probably told ya'll she's pregnant. Let's go." Lo tugged her arm, and she stumbled behind him, looking over her shoulder at us.

"We're talking later, Gwen," she vowed, determination lacing her voice.

Cyn stood up, stretching her back as she walked out of the bathroom. "She's right, by the way. You're not getting out of this that easy." Cyn winked at me and made her way back over to the table, sliding in next to Rigid. He wrapped his arm around her and pulled her close, whispering in her ear.

I smiled, seeing the love between the two and knowing they were going to be incredible parents.

I glanced at Gambler, his back turned to me and breathed a heavy sigh. Uh. What the hell was I doing with Gambler? I liked him. I truly did.

Gambler turned around, his eyes searching for me. I flicked off the bathroom light and made my way back to the table. His eyes watched me the whole way, studying the way I walked, his eyes flaring as I put a little more sway in my walk.

I had enough. I wanted Gambler. I knew, right then and there, that this man might hurt me, but he was going to be worth the pain.

''*'*'*'*'*'*'*'*

Chapter 12

GAMBLER

We were cruising down the road, the wind cutting through me and Gwen was pressed to my back, holding on. We had just left the restaurant and pulled on the highway, King leading us to the pumpkin place. I never thought I would say that I was going to a pumpkin patch, but here I was. Marley and Troy were meeting us there and planned on hauling all the pumpkins back in Troy's truck.

Before we had gotten on the bike, I had handed Gwen her helmet, but she didn't grab it. "What are we doing, Gambler?"

"We gotta get on the road, doll. Put the helmet on."

"That's not what I meant. I mean, what are we," she pointed between the two if us, "what the hell is going on?"

I stared down at her, helmet in between us. Jesus, I didn't expect that question. I was still trying to figure out what the hell we were and now Gwen wanted to know. "Um, well, I'm not sure."

"You're not sure?"

"Well, what are you thinking?"

She glanced to the left and cleared her throat. "I'm not sure either," she mumbled.

I threw my head back, laughing at the fact that she also had no idea what the hell was going on between us. Although when it came down to it, we both knew what was going on, we were just fighting it tooth and nail. "God dammit, I fucking like you, Gwen. I don't know what the hell to do with that, but I fucking like you."

Gwen turned her head back to me, her eyes laughing at me. "You fucking like me?"

"Yeah."

"Well," she pushed her blowing hair out of her face and smiled. "I fucking like you, too, Gambler. Half the time I don't know if I wanna kick you in the shin, or kiss you till you shut up."

"We can try the second option first," I smirked, pulling her into my arms. The helmet was sandwiched between us, but I had Gwen in my arms, somewhat.

"I know you're going to hurt me, Gambler. Hopefully, we can make some good memories for when the pain sets in I have something to remember you," she whispered.

"I got no plans of hurting you, Gwen, but I can promise I'll give you as many good memories as possible." I leaned down, my lips brushing against hers. She reached for the helmet and tossed it on the ground.

"Let's make one right now," she whispered, reaching up, threading her fingers through my hair. Her lips touched mine, and I knew I was a goner. If being with Gwen was going to feel like this, I didn't know what the hell I was thinking running from her before.

"Woo!" I heard yelled from behind us. I deepened the kiss, not wanting to let Gwen go. She moaned low, her body pressed against mine. My dick begged to be buried in her sweet pussy after only kissing her. Once I got her naked, Lord knows what would happen.

"Told ya something was going on," Cyn said, cutting into our little world.

Gwen pulled away, her lips wet and tempting. I pressed one last kiss to them, reminding myself that there was always later. She let go of my hair, trailing her fingers down my shirt, sending shivers down my spine at her words. "I'm gonna need more later," she purred, her eyes filled with desire.

"As soon as we're done with this pumpkin shit, there'll be more, doll. So much more." She backed away from me, her eyes studying me as she grabbed the helmet off the ground and strapped it on.

"Promises, promises, Gambler. Let's hope you can keep all of them."

I heard King crank his bike up, and I knew it was time to go. I swung my leg over my bike, not even having to wait five seconds before I felt Gwen's warm body pressed against mine.

"How long until we get there?" Gwen called over the roar of the motorcycle.

"About half an hour," I said, turning my head so she could hear me.

I felt her hands sneak into the pockets of my jacket, pressing against my stomach.

"My hands are cold," she mumbled into my ear and burrowed into my back. It was rather cold to be out riding today, and I knew this would probably be one of the last times Gwen and I rode this year before the snow started falling.

We were five miles away from our exit when I noticed a black van behind us, weaving in and out of traffic. King and Rigid were a few car lengths ahead of us, riding side by side.

Just as I glanced in my mirror to see where the van was, I saw an arm reach out the passenger side window, a gun pointed at Gwen and me.

I swerved to the left, then to the right, knowing if I kept moving they wouldn't be able to get a shot off at us.

"Gambler?" I heard Gwen call, panic in her voice. I didn't want to worry her, but I didn't know what the hell we were dealing with. I speed up, taking the shoulder around the car in front of us, the van also going faster and squeezing itself through two cars, keeping up alongside me. I slowed down, not wanting the van to catch up to King and Rigid. The van slowed down with us, the car that was separating us slamming on its brakes when the guy in the van pulled the gun out again, pointing it at us. I speed up, zig-zagging, trying to lose the van. Gwen's arms tightened around me, holding on as I went faster and faster, trying to shake the van.

I could tell the two guys in the van were getting impatient when they swerved at us, attempting to run us off the road.

I heard two gun shots and looked over, the guy now taking aim at my tires, trying to make me wreck.

We were a mile from our exit, and I knew I had to do something. Just as I was about to slam on the brakes, I heard another shot fired from the gun and I felt a sharp, burning sting in my leg. I glanced down, blood staining my jeans. Shit.

"Gambler!" Gwen screeched as I revved the throttle, knowing I need to get off the road. All I remember was hearing one more shot and then the world went dark as I felt a stabbing pain in my neck and prayed to God that I didn't kill Gwen. The world went dark and the pain faded.

''*'*'*'*'*'*'*'*'*'

Chapter 13

Gwen

I don't know how, but I swear to God I could feel Gambler getting shot.

When Gambler had first started swerving, I had no idea what he was doing. I thought maybe he was trying to scare me a bit, not knowing that I had been on a motorcycle many times before.

I finally realized what was going on when the black van sped up, and a gun came out of the window, attached to a very pissed off Mexican man.

When Gambler's body had gone limp, I knew I had to do something or we were going to crash, bad. I reach for the handlebars, squashing Gambler. I knocked his hands off the handlebars, the fact that he had let go so easily scared the shit out of me, but I knew I couldn't focus on that right now. My hands gripped the bars just as the bike started to shake and sway. I tried coasting to a stop, avoiding traffic and causing an even worse accident than we were about to have.

I bumped over to the shoulder, rocks kicking up under the tires. I hit the brakes, and I knew as soon as I did it, I had made a mistake. The wheels skidded, and I tried to correct it, but I couldn't.

We skidded, leaning over to the left, and I saw the road come up and rip my leg apart, feeling like burning coals as the gravel and dirt embedded in my leg. I let go of the handlebars and held onto Gambler. The bike skidded ahead of us as Gambler and I rolled into the ditch. My head banged on the road, thankfully protected by the helmet Gambler insisted I always wear.

When we finally came to a stop, my arms were still wrapped around his body I heard him moan, and I thanked God that he was still alive. We had both just laid the bike down, but he had also been shot, maybe twice.

I heard the screeching of tires, and I immediately panicked, thinking that whoever had shot at us had come to finish the job.

"Call nine one one, now!" I heard bellowed. I craned my neck, trying to see who was talking, but we were too far down in the ditch to see the road. Two sets of black boots came stomping down the embankment skidding to a stop next to Gambler and me.

I held Gambler tight to me and closed my eyes, afraid to see who had found us. "Gwen, it's us darlin', nothing is going to happen to ya'll. Meg is calling an ambulance right now." I opened my eyes and looked up into King's face.

"Thank God," I cried.

"Where are you hurt? Did you get shot?" Rigid asked, kneeling on the other side of me.

"Um, I'm hurt, but Gambler was shot. Once for sure in the neck, and I think in the leg too. You have to help him!"

"We will, darlin'. You're gonna have to let him go, though." Rigid said, prying my arms away from Gambler. I didn't realize how tight I had been holding on to him until I tried loosening my arms and my muscles relaxed, crying out in relief.

"Can you move?" King asked me.

I took stock of my body, trying to figure out if anything was broken. I was bleeding, bruised, and sore, but I didn't think anything was broken. "I think I'm OK," I said hoarsely.

"I just want you to lie here until the ambulance comes." Rigid gently lifted Gambler off of me and laid him next to me. Gambler's eyes fluttered open and I cried out, thankful he was conscious.

Rigid looked at his neck, trying to see how bad he had been hit. "I think it just grazed him. I'm not sure, but it doesn't look like there is an entry wound."

"What about his leg?" I asked, trying to sit up, but my arms shook and I collapsed onto the ground.

"Gwen, you need to just lay down," King ordered. He undid the helmet on my head, gently taking it off. He took off his coat, folded it up and slid it under my head. "Stay still."

"The ambulance will be here in five minutes," Meg called.

"I want you and Cyn to stay up there and wait for it to come. It might miss us if we're all down here," King called.

"Is everyone OK?"

"Gwen is banged up, and Gambler got shot. He's losing a lot of blood; we need to get him out of here as fast as we can."

Gambler groaned, and I tried to get up again, but King held me down. "I'm not going to tell you again, Gwen. Stay still. There could be something wrong with you that we can't see. Stay. Still."

"She's stubborn as shit," Gambler wheezed.

"Gambler," I cried. I had never been so relieved to hear his voice before.

"Gwen," he gasped.

"Stop trying to talk, brother. The ambulance should be here any minute." Rigid pressed down on his shoulder when he attempted to sit up. "Stop trying to move. I don't know what's all wrong with ya'll."

"My ribs." Gambler moved his hand, grasping his left side. That was the side we had fallen on. I tried to hold onto Gambler as much as I could, but I knew he had taken the brunt of the fall.

"Probably broke a few. Just lay still. If you move wrong, you might puncture a lung."

King stood up and walked over to the edge of the ditch. "I hear sirens, babe. You see it yet?"

"I see cars pulling over up there." I heard Meg say.

"There it is!" Cyn called.

The next ten minutes were a whirlwind of poking, prodding, and twenty questions. As they were loading Gambler up onto a gurney, another ambulance arrived to take me to the hospital. Gambler was still conscious and answering questions the whole time. He tried insisting that I go in the first ambulance but the paramedics ignored him and loaded him up while he protested.

"All right, we're going to slide this board under you, and then we'll get you loaded up." I glanced to the left, watching the woman paramedic who had been talking to me the whole time, explaining everything as it happened.

"We're going to the same hospital as Gambler, right?"

"Gambler? You mean the other guy who was just here? Of course. We'll try to get ya'll in close rooms, too, as long as he doesn't need to be on a different floor." The paramedic finished writing on her clipboard and shoved it into her bag. "Just stay still and relax. As far we can tell there isn't any internal bleeding."

I was hoisted up and carried over to the ambulance and raised in. "We'll meet you at the hospital," Meg called as the back doors slammed shut.

I closed my eyes, trying not to worry about Gambler. They had figured that he had broken a couple of ribs from the fall and, of course, other bumps, bruises, and cuts. He was just grazed by the bullet on his neck and his leg didn't appear to have hit any major arteries. We were both OK for the most part.

I felt the ambulance pull off the shoulder and head to the hospital. Somehow a day of relaxing fun had turned into ambulance rides and gun shots.

''*'*'*'*'*'*'*'*'*'*

Chapter 14

GAMBLER

"I need to know how Gwen is. I don't care about me. Just tell me if she's OK," I pleaded with the nurse who was taking my blood pressure.

"I can't say anything about other patients unless you are family. I told you once you're up to it and if she agrees, I'll take you over to see her." The nurse scribbled something down on her clipboard and clipped it to the end of the bed and walked out of the room.

I had been here for over an hour, and I hadn't been able to find out any information on Gwen. King had come, and I told him to not come back until he had information on Gwen. I was afraid he was running into the same problem I was, none of us were her family.

I glanced around the room and spotted the phone next to the bed. I knew what I was about to do was a longshot, but I didn't have much choice.

I picked up the receiver and called the front desk of the hospital.

"Rockton General, how may I direct your call?"

"I need to speak to a Gwen Lawson. She was in a car accident today. I'm her brother."

"Hold please." The line clicked over to cheesy jazz music, and I waited for two minutes before she came back on the line.

"We have her in room two fourteen. Would you like me to ring you over to her room?"

Hell yeah! "Yes, please." The shit music came back on, but this time, I didn't mind it because I knew the next person I talked to was going to be Gwen.

"Hello?" Jesus, freakin' Meg.

"Put Gwen on the phone."

"Gambler? What the hell are you doing calling? Aren't you in a room just down the hall?"

"Yeah, but they won't tell me anything about Gwen. I called pretending to be her brother and they patched me over to her room. Put her on the phone."

"Jeez, desperate much?" she scoffed. "Gambler wants you," I heard Meg say as she handed the phone to Gwen.

"Gambler?" Gwen asked, surprised.

"It's me, doll. The damn nurse won't tell me how you are doing so I got creative and rang the front desk and said I was your brother."

Gwen laughed, "You must have been desperate."

"I just need to know if you're OK, doll."

"I'm OK. Just bumps and bruises. My leg is pretty shredded, but it's all superficial. I think I'll be out of here in a little bit. What about you?"

I adjusted the blanket that was draped over me and slowly raised my other arm over my head, careful not to hurt my neck. There was an enormous bandage on the left side of my neck where the bullet had ripped open my skin. The doctor had said if it had hit me a half an inch to left I wouldn't be here anymore. "I'm hanging in there. I think I'm going to need to spend the night tonight, but I should be out of here in the morning."

"Oh crap, the nurse just came in. I'll call you back. What room are you in?"

I looked around, trying to see a room number. "I don't know, doll. I'll call you back in twenty minutes, that ok?" I don't know why I needed to call her back. I had found out that she was OK, that was all I needed to know.

"OK. Bye," she whispered. The dial tone of the phone sounded in my ear, and I replaced the receiver on the table.

Now, what the hell was I supposed to do? I glanced at the clock, seeing it was only half past three. I flipped the TV on, flipping through the channels till I found a marathon of *Fast and Loud*. Hammer, Slider, and Gravel had stopped by earlier but had left to go scope out the cafeteria for any good food. I told them they were on a hopeless mission, but they still went.

I glanced at the clock again, seeing it had only been five minutes since I talked to Gwen. I laid my head back on the pillow and watched the TV waiting for fifteen minutes to go by. Not even ten minutes later I was passed out, the medicine they had given me finally kicking in. I never got to call Gwen back.

''*'*'*'*'*'*'*'*'*'*

Chapter 15

Gwen

"Are you sure you want us to leave you here?"

I glanced over my shoulder at Marley and Troy, who were standing behind me in the hallway.

"Yeah, I'll be fine. Hell, the hospital is probably the safest place for me." I had just been released and was standing in the door to Gambler's room. He had never called me back, and I was worried that something had happened to him. Thankfully all that had happened to him was that he fell asleep.

"Do you want me to bring you some more clothes?" I glanced down at the yoga pants and shirt Marley had in Troy's truck and shook my head.

"I'll be fine. Gambler said he should be released tomorrow so this will be fine until then." Thankfully the pants were stretchy enough I could squeeze my ass into them and the shirt was baggy.

"OK, well, I guess we'll see you tomorrow. Call me if you need anything, OK?" Marley said, her voice laced with concern.

"Will do. I think we all just need to relax." I glanced back into Gambler's room, seeing he was still sleeping.

"Troy has to head to work, but remember, if you need me, just call." Marley wrapped her arms around me, squeezing the hell out of me. "I'm so glad you're OK," she whispered.

I hugged her back, thankful that today wasn't as bad as it could have been. "Me too," I said, stepping back. Troy threw his arm over her shoulder, and they walked down the hall arm in arm.

I stepped into the room, mindful of being quiet as I shut the door and looked around. His room was set up just like mine was, and I walked over to the chair that was next to the bed. I sat down gingerly and stretched my legs out in front of me. My leg protested pain shooting up it and I grimaced. Fuck that hurt. My leg didn't hurt that bad until they had washed it out and scrubbed it clean of all the dirt and gravel. Now it was tender and painful.

There was a knock on the door and the same nurse who had taken care of me walked in the room. She looked at me in surprise and smiled. "I should have known you would come down here." She walked over to the sink and washed her hands.

"I wanted to make sure he was OK," I said meekly, afraid she was going to tell me I had to leave.

She grabbed paper towels and dried her hands as she studied me. "You're fine, hun. No need to look like I'm the bouncer about to kick you out," she laughed. She grabbed his chart from the bottom of the bed, and I breathed a sigh of relief. "That chair you're sitting in folds down into a bed. Probably not the comfiest, but it'll be better than the floor," she said as she studied the chart. She grabbed her pen out of her pocket and scribbled something down.

"It'll be OK if I spend the night?"

"Of course, hun. Just no parties," she winked at me and walked over to the machines that were hooked up to Gambler.

"He's going to be OK, right?"

"As far as I can tell he should be good. It'll take a bit to recover, but nothing I don't think he can't handle." She scribbled something on the clipboard and looked up at me. "How long have you two been together? He was asking to see you the whole time, too."

"Oh, well, I'm not really sure we're even together." I looked down at my hands clasped in my hands and bit my lip. Jeez, this was such a messed up situation.

"Oh, well, maybe ya'll figure things out now." She smiled at me sympathetically, setting the clipboard at the end of the bed and walked out of the room, quietly shutting the door.

Figure things out? Lord knew if that would happen. When Gambler had passed out on the bike, I had panicked thinking the worse, and as much as I tried to tell myself that didn't mean anything, I couldn't deny it anymore. Gambler meant something to me. The way I felt about him was something new and scary.

I grabbed the remote from the side of the bed and turned up the volume. He was watching some car show I had never seen before, but you really couldn't go wrong with hot guys and cars.

After two episodes, my stomach started growling, and I was seriously considering wandering around in search of food.

Just as I grabbed my wallet off the floor, Gambler stirred next to me, his head turning towards the door. I watched his hand as he flexed his fingers, and I wondered if he was awake.

"Shit," he cursed his voice gravely from sleep.

Well, that answered my question. He turned his head to the table beside me and looked at the time. "Fuck."

"Is something wrong?" I asked.

His eyes shot to me, "What the hell?"

"Um, did you need something?" I had no idea what he meant by 'what the hell.' Maybe he didn't expect me to be here or he didn't want me here.

"I forgot to call you." He cleared his throat, and his eyes traveled all over my body, taking in my less than stellar appearance and baggy clothes.

"Oh, that's OK. I might have missed it if you had called. I got discharged right after I got off the phone with you." I clasped my hands in my lap, searching for what else to say.

"You're OK to go home?"

"So they say. My leg is pretty beaten up, but I'm good. I'm sure tomorrow I'll be pretty stiff."

"I think stiff might be an understatement, doll," he winked at me, his gorgeous smile spreading across his lips.

"You might be right although you might have it a bit worse than me." I motioned to the bandage on his neck and felt the tears coming. I had no idea why I was about to cry. I think it was finally hitting me that today could have turned out a lot worse than it did.

I glanced away, my eyes trying to focus on the TV, but they were blurred by the tears that I couldn't hold back. I tried swiping them away as they rained down my cheeks, but there were too many to catch.

My world felt like it was about to end, and I had no idea how to stop it. Gambler was OK, I kept reminding myself.

"Gwen," Gambler quietly called to me. All I could do was shake my head and sob. "Gwen, come here."

"I... can't," I hiccupped.

"I need to hold you right now, Gwen. Don't make me get out of this bed. I think I'd be pretty shaky right now."

Deep breaths. Everything and everyone was fine. I counted backward from ten trying to calm the panic that was trying to overtake me.

"Son of a bitch," Gambler grumbled under his breath.

I saw him toss the blanket off him and try to swing his legs out of the bed. "What the hell are you doing?" I demanded, shooting up from my chair.

"You need me, and I can't fucking get to you right now." He tried to sit up and grimaced in pain, holding his stomach.

"Gambler, stop it!" I gently pushed on his shoulder and grabbed the corner of the blanket he had tossed off. I pulled it up over his legs, noticing the large bandage on his leg, but blocked from my mind how he had gotten it. "You don't need to worry about me right now," I scolded, tucking him back in.

"Get in here with me," he ordered, tossing back the blanket again.

"No, you're crazy. You need to rest, not have me smushed in that bed with you."

"I'm not taking no for an answer, doll. I want you in this bed with me. I may not be able to do what I really wanted to do to you the next time I had you in bed, but I can still damn sure hold you."

"Gambler, I can't. I'm-"

"Gwen, get in the fucking bed." I looked him in the eye, and I knew he wasn't messing around.

"Gambler, if I hurt you by climbing in that bed, I don't think I'll be able to live with myself."

"You won't hurt me," he grabbed my hand, tugging me closer to the bed. "I need to make sure you're fine, and the only way it's going to sink in that we're both alive and not dead is if I hold you in my arms. I need you right now, Gwen."

The tears sprung back, swelling and building. "I need you, too," I choked out.

I slipped off my shoes, tucking them under the bed, and pulled the covers back more. Gambler slowly slid over to the other side of the bed gingerly. I slid in, clinging to the edge of the bed, afraid to touch him.

"Gwen, you better get your ass next to me in two seconds, or you can guarantee when I'm feeling better I'll bend you over my knee and spank that pretty ass."

"You can try," I scoffed, scooting over next to him.

His shirt was off and I cuddled up under his arm he was holding out and rested my head against his shoulder, mindful of his neck. "How bad does it hurt?" I asked, looking up at him.

His head was tilted down, his eyes studying me. "I'm pretty doped up right now, doll. I don't feel much."

I pinched his side, and he jumped under my touch. "What the hell did you do that for?"

"Just wanted to see if you would feel it," I laughed, leaning up, brushing a kiss on his cheek.

"You're crazy. They sure you don't have a concussion?" He rubbed his side and smiled at me.

"Positive," I mumbled. "So, are you going to tell me what the hell that was today, or am I going to have to pump Meg for information?" I rested my head back on his shoulder and traced over his tattoos on his chest with my fingertips.

"We don't know much, yet. I know it was the Assassins, but we don't know why they went after you and I. Their main beef has always been with Rigid, but they could have confused me with him today, or, they could just be going after anyone with the Devil's Knights patch."

"So this isn't over yet?" I asked, worried that something worse could happen next time.

"I don't think so, doll. I know King was going to put a couple of calls in and see what he can find out."

"So now we sit like ducks waiting to be attacked again."

"This isn't going to happen again. This is the last time the Assassins are going to get the jump on us."

I snuggled deeper into Gambler's arms, feeling safer than I should. Even though I knew there was no way for him to guarantee to keep us safe, I knew he would die trying. "I trust you, Gambler," I whispered.

He leaned over, burying his nose in my hair and breathed a sigh of relief. "You have no idea how much that means to me, doll."

I did know how much it meant because I never trusted anyone. Gambler was the first in a very long time who I had given my trust to. I just prayed that I wasn't wrong.

''*'*'*'*'*'*'*'*'*'*'*'*

Chapter 16

GAMBLER

"Woman, for the last freakin' time, I'm all right!"

"No, you're not! It's only been two weeks since you were shot! There is no way you are driving your bike today." Gwen crossed her arms over her chest, pushing up her tits that were already hanging out of her shirt.

We had just woken up, and she was driving me crazy with her rumpled, sexy hair and sleepy look on her face. Although, right now she was more pissed off than sleepy. It had been over two weeks since we had crashed, and I was about to go fucking crazy.

Don't get me wrong, I loved Gwen fawning over me, but sometimes a man needed a rest. She had insisted I not ride my bike whenever we need to go anywhere, and I had been OK with that for a while, but now I was done with it.

I pulled a shirt out of my dresser and pulled it over my head. "Gwen, I'm going. I need to go."

She was sitting in the middle of the bed, arms crossed looking like a pissed off vixen. Every minute I spent with her, the more I didn't want to let her go. We didn't fight and argue at every turn anymore, but it wasn't like much else had changed.

It was almost like we were in limbo, each waiting for the other one to make a move.

"It's too cold to go for a ride, anyway. It's fifty degrees out. You'll freeze your balls off."

"Not like I'm using them," I mumbled under my breath as I grabbed my cut off the chair and pulled it on. I tossed open the door to the closet and grabbed my leather jacket out.

OK, so another reason I was ready to get the fuck out of here was Gwen. I had never had such a case of blue balls in my life. She drove me crazy with her short shorts and tank tops she wore to bed. Then rubbing all over me while she slept and woke up like she just hadn't basically molested me while she slept. Don't even get me started on what she wore when she was awake.

"Well, then I'm coming with you," Gwen crawled to the end of the bed, her sweet tits swaying under her barely their tank top, and I couldn't take it anymore.

"Stop!" She froze, balancing on all fours, her shocked face staring at me. "Get your ass back in bed, and I'll be back later. I'm taking Roam and Slider with me. I'll be fine." I stormed out of the room, the door banging against the door as I walked down the hall.

I couldn't take it anymore. She had to know what she was doing to me. I was a man with only so much self-control before I would snap. I needed to make her mine, but I'd be damned if that was what she wanted. She treated me like a fucking friend, not like someone she wanted to fuck the shit out of.

"Let's go," I growled, walking past Slider and Roam, who were drinking coffee at the bar. They both set their cups down and followed me out the door, no questions asked. All the guys could tell I was ready to fucking explode each time they talked to me.

I tossed my leg over my bike, knowing all eyes were on me, but I didn't fucking care. Ninety percent of these fuckers were getting pussy every night while I laid in my bed every night with the most gorgeous woman I had ever known and woke up with blue balls every morning.

"Where we headed?" Slider asked, walking over to his bike.

"Not a fucking clue. I just need to clear my head." I cranked up my bike, not waiting for a response. I just needed to drive and not think. I looked over my shoulder making sure Roam was ready to go. Slider and Roam both cranked up their bikes and it was finally time to get the fuck out of here.

I headed out of town, not knowing where the hell I was headed but thankful to be headed where ever the hell it was. I needed to ride till I forgot the past two weeks and maybe ride Gwen out of my system.

Who the fuck knew how long that would take. That woman had made me her's, and she hadn't even touched me yet. What the fuck?

''*'*'*'*'*'*'*'*'*'*

Gwen

I sat in the middle of the rumpled bed wondering what the hell just happened. I was only trying to help. Gambler was hurt, and I was just trying to go out of my way to make him comfortable.

I could tell the past couple of days he was growing restless, but I guess I didn't know how much.

"Hey, where the hell did Gambler head off to?" Meg asked, walking into the room.

"Um, not sure," I mumbled, wiping the tears that had been flowing down my cheeks.

"Hey, what the hell is wrong?" she asked, sitting on the end of the bed.

"Oh, nothing. I guess I must have gotten on Gambler's nerves."

Meg jumped and grabbed the box of kleenex out of the bathroom and handed them to me. "I'm sure he just needed a break, babe. Don't stress over it."

"It's kind of hard not to when he just yelled at me. It's just that things have been almost strained between us these past few weeks. I have no idea what to say or do around him. The only time things seem to be chill between us is when we are in bed."

"Oh, well, at least, you've got the whole sex thing going for you." Meg winked at me and plopped down on the bed, laying down across the foot of the bed.

"Please, we cuddle, that's it," I scoffed. I blew my nose and wiped my eyes and tossed the box of Kleenex on the nightstand. I turned back to Meg and her jaw was hanging wide open.

"You mean to tell me all you guys do is sleep? What the hell happened between the parking lot of the restaurant and now? You both looked like you were ready to rip each other's clothes off that day."

"I have no idea what happened. It's like I just freeze around him. I want him so fucking bad, but I have no idea how to tell him. I spend so much time with him you would think that I would just be able to say it, but I can't. I'm one of those chicks I can't stand who want something but don't know how to go after it." I grabbed a pillow from the head of the bed and set it on my lap.

"I think you should just rip his clothes off the next time you see him and he'll take the rest from there."

"I'm pretty sure that's what it's all going to come down to." My phone rang, and I grabbed it off the nightstand and saw it was Paige calling. "I gotta take this, it's my sister," I mumbled as I swiped left and put the phone to my ear. Meg waved her hand at me and grabbed her phone out of her pocket and started texting someone.

"Hello?"

"Are you sure you're ready for me to move to Rockton?"

"I am more than ready. When do you leave?"

"Let's see, today is Friday, and I have about two or three more days of packing, so I hope to be there by Wednesday at the latest."

"It's about freakin' time. I let Aunt Rose know last week you were coming. She's over the moon to have us both back in the same town again."

"I can't wait to see her. So, how's it going with your motorcycle man?"

Ugh, not this again. I never should have told Paige about Gambler. I didn't really see any way around it, though. "There's not much to tell."

"Ha! I don't believe that for a second. I'm sure you've got him eating out of your hand already. I can't wait to meet the man who finally made you settle down."

I wouldn't really say I was settled down. I mean, I was living in the clubhouse of a motorcycle club. Not exactly settled. "It's nothing, Paige."

"Hmm, well, I guess I'll just have to be the judge of that when I get there."

"Ugh, there's nothing to judge."

"Suuure. Well, I need to get back to packing. I just wanted to make sure you still wanted me up there before I start packing all my Mary Moo Moo's."

Oh, jeez. "Pack the Mary Moo Moo's. There's no turning back after you do. Call me Monday."

I hung the phone up and tossed it on the bed.

"What the fuck is a Mary Moo Moo?" Meg asked, her eyes as big as saucers.

I burst out laughing realizing I probably sounded crazy talking to Paige. "They're these figurines of cows that my sister collects."

"Who the hell collects figurines of cows?"

"Um, Paige and my aunt apparently," I laughed.

"Oh, well. That's different. I'll have to check out her cows when she gets into town."

"I'll let her know to expect you," I laughed.

"You up to blowing this pop stand today?" Meg asked, sitting up.

"I guess." I had no idea when Gambler was going to be back, so I suppose it was probably good to be distracted and not mope around all day.

"I just texted Cyn and Marley and asked if they wanted to go to the mall. They're down. Lo and Rigid are going to come along, too."

"OK, just let me get dressed and grab a cup of coffee." I scooted out of the bed and walked over to my suitcase that was in the corner. I really needed to get my clothes out of this suitcase but I was too scared to ask Gambler if I could use some closet space.

"I'm gonna go make some more coffee." Meg rolled off the bed and straightened her shirt. "I wouldn't worry about Gambler, Gwen. I'm pretty sure you just scare the shit out of him and he has no idea what to do."

"Well, I hope you're right." I flipped open the suitcase and started rummaging through it, trying to find something that wasn't too wrinkled. "I'll meet you in the kitchen in a couple of minutes." Meg walked out, leaving the door open and headed down the hall.

I sat back on my butt and wondered what the hell I was going to do. I obviously needed to do something different than what I had been doing.

Gambler knew I liked him, so I had no idea why the hell it was so hard for us to be together.

I had been hurt in the past by so many douchebags that I was definitely hesitant to let go, but I knew that Gambler was going to be worth any heartbreak.

I grabbed my black leggings and red button down shirt that had tiny black polka dots all over it and tossed it on the bed. I pulled out my other suitcase out from under the bed looking for the perfect shoes. I was in a shitty mood, so I needed to dress to the nines to make myself feel better. My four-inch patent leather heels called to me as I grabbed them and knew these were going to be just the thing to get me out of this funk.

I grabbed my clothes and shoes and headed into the bathroom, stripped down, and hopped into the shower. I quickly washed, shampooed, and conditioned and was out in record time. I knew everyone was waiting for me, so I blew out my hair and tied it back with a red bandana. Did a quick swipe of mascara, eyeliner, and eyeshadow and topped everything off with my favorite lip gloss.

As I slipped my feet into my heels, they gave me a confidence I hadn't had in a while.

I stood up, looking at myself in the mirror and smiled. It was time to take the plunge with Gambler.

''*'*'*'*'*'*'*'*'*

Chapter 17

GAMBLER

I should have known that I would end up here. I hadn't been by to visit Evie in a while. Slider and Roam had held back at the bottom of the hill, knowing I needed time alone. We had driven for over an hour before I realized I was headed straight here.

Her stone was covered with fallen leaves and dead grass. I pulled off my leather glove and used it to brush the stone off. The flowers I had laid there last time were gone and replaced by bright pink daisies my mom always left. She must have been here in the past couple of days. She was always better at getting out here to see Evie than I was.

"I'm sorry I haven't been out here in a while, Evie. I was in an accident a couple of weeks ago and Gwen had me on a short leash." I looked up at the sky, regret washing over me like it did each time I came here. I should get out to see her every week, but life always seemed to get in the way.

"I don't know what to do with her, Evie. I wish you were here to help me figure things out. You always were the one who told me if a girl was worth it or not. You had that special sense to you." I had always had Evie meet my girlfriends and knew she would give it to me straight about them. Ninety-nine percent of them she told me to let them go. She was right, too. There was only one girl she ever told me was worth it, but it turned out that girl didn't think I was worth it. Go figure.

"She scares the fucking shit out of me, Evie. I've never been with someone who makes me want to give them everything. I'm pretty sure I'd die just to see her beautiful smile one more time." I knelt down, my knee sinking into the wet ground, soaking through my jeans. "When we crashed, all I could think was if anything happened to Gwen, I wouldn't be able to go on." My heart squeezed in my chest just thinking about Gwen dying. The last time I had ever felt that kind of pain was when Evie had died. "I need to let her go, but I fucking can't. I feel like I'll drown in her and never want to come up for air. She's going to destroy me either way." I bowed my head down, a fucking tear streaking down my cheek.

The wind picked up, swirling the fallen leaves around me and the chill cut through my leather jacket, reminding me that it really wasn't the best weather to be riding, but I needed to clear my head. "Maybe I should have mom meet her. I haven't been by to see her in over a month." I tried to get out to see mom at least once a month, but just like with visiting Evie, life got in the way. I pulled my phone out of my pocket and dialed my mom.

She picked up on the second ring, her voice eager to hear from me. "Anthony?"

"Yeah, it's me, Ma. I'm up here with Evie." I pulled the collar of my coat tighter around me, realizing Gwen might have been right about going for a ride today.

"Oh, I was just up there to see her two days ago. I talked to Hank about keeping her grave cleaner. He said he would personally make sure it wouldn't be such a mess the next time I came up."

"It was pretty good when I came today. Just some leaves." Keeping Evie's grave clear and clean was my mother's number one vice. I think she felt that it was the one way she could still feel connected to Evie and protect her.

"Good, good. How are you? I haven't heard from you in a while. The occasional text or call would not go underappreciated."

"I know, Ma. I was actually calling to see if you would want to have dinner next week with Gwen and me."

"Gwen? Who is Gwen?" Her voice peaked with curiosity, and I knew she was dying to know what was going on. I had never mentioned anyone to her since Evie had passed.

"Um, well, I think she's a girl I'm seeing." I ran my fingers through my hair and winced at how stupid I sounded. I was thirty-seven years old, and I didn't even know if I was seeing someone.

"Oh my," she whispered. "This is huge for you, Anthony."

"I know, Ma. I don't know what the hell I'm doing. I came to see Evie hoping she would give me answers, but talking to a stone only makes me look crazy."

"Oh, Anthony, you don't look crazy. You go there for the same reason I do. You feel close to her for a little bit, but it also helps you to get things out. It helps to clear my head when I go out there. When Evie was alive, when I talked to her I felt the same way. She was always the best listener."

I thought about what my mom had just said, and she was right. Although I didn't get an answer from Evie, I got all my thoughts out. All the things that were bothering me were now laid out before me, and I could see things more clearly. "She did always listen, Ma, but as soon as you were done she let you know what she thought," I laughed.

"She sure did." My mom went quiet, thinking about Evie. "I'd love to meet your Gwen, Anthony. I'm sure I'll love her. If she's good enough to capture your attention, she had to be pretty special."

"She's definitely something else." I shook my head, realizing Gwen drove me crazy, but I fucking loved it. "We'll be out Thursday night, that ok?"

"It's perfect. I'll make sure to get home early from work and make something special."

"Don't go to too much trouble, Ma. I know you're tired when you get off of work." Ma was a school counselor and treated each and every one of those kids like they were her own.

"Don't worry about it. Just be here by six. That will give me plenty of time."

"Alright, Ma, I'll see you then." I hung the phone up and shoved it into my pocket. I stood up, brushing the grass off my jeans and ran my fingers through my hair.

"I really wish you were here, Evie. I think you'd really like Gwen. I'll be back in a couple of weeks." I walked away from her grave and down the hill where Slider and Roam were waiting for me.

"You 'aight, brother?" Roam asked.

"Nothing a bottle of Jack and a couple hands of poker can't fix," I laughed.

"Who was she to you?" Slider asked, nodding up the hill.

I glanced over my shoulder at where I just came from and sighed. I've never really told any of the newer brothers about Evie. King, Demon, Gravel, and Roam knew about her, but that was it. "She's my sister. Died 6 years ago."

"Sorry, man."

"Yeah, me too." I walked over to my bike and swung my leg over and glanced at Roam and Slider. "You guys good for driving for a bit longer?"

"I got nothing but time, brother. You lead, we'll follow. We know you got shit bugging ya right now," Roam replied, saying exactly the right thing.

This was what I loved about this club. Even when it was freezing fucking cold, my brothers were there for me, riding around so I could sort my head out. "We'll just take the long way home. I pissed Gwen off when I left, and I should probably get back sooner rather than later."

"King texted me and said they were all headed to the mall. He said Demon was keeping an eye on Gwen."

"Demon?" Roam nodded his head, a shit eating grin spreading across his face. "I'm sure he'll take good care of her while you're gone."

Motherfucker. What the hell was that supposed to mean? Demon didn't like Gwen. Hell, even if he did, he better keep his fucking hands off of Gwen. "What time did he text you?"

"He must have texted me about fifteen minutes after we took off. I'm sure everything is fine, brother. He can't do much with her at the mall."

"He better not do anything with her!" I roared, pissed the fuck off. I hadn't even had the chance to make her mine and already I was going to have to mark my fucking territory. "Demon knows I'm with Gwen."

"Then you shouldn't have anything to worry about as long as Gwen knows that, too." Slider slipped his sunglasses on his face and smirked at me.

"You're both fuckers, you know that, right?" I cranked up my bike and headed out the gate. It was going to take at least an hour to get back to Gwen.

"Yo! I need to stop for gas!" Roam yelled at me.

I waved my hand at him, letting him know I had heard. Fuck me, better make that over an hour to get home now.

Demon better know that Gwen was mine. If he didn't, I'd sure as shit let him know. No one was touching Gwen but me.

*ʾ*ʾ*ʾ*ʾ*ʾ*ʾ*ʾ*ʾ*

Chapter 18

Gwen

"That'll be two hundred thirty-seven dollars and fifteen cents," the cashier said. I forked over the money and grabbed the four bags she handed me. "Have a nice day."

"You too," I mumbled, shocked by the fact on how much I had just spent at Victoria's Secret. I figured out what her secret was. The shit was fucking expensive.

"Lo is going to flip when he sees what I bought. He isn't going to know what hit him," Meg purred, peaking into her bag.

"Ugh, I hate you both. I couldn't buy anything because I'm about to blow up into a whale," Cyn groaned, standing up from the bench that was outside the store.

"You could have come in with us," Meg chided, looping her arm through Megs. "Preggo can still be sexy." She leaned down and rubbed Cyn's belly

Cyn swatted her hand away and rolled her eyes. "All I feel right now is bloated. Bloated is not sexy."

"I bet Rigid still thinks you're sexy," Marley said, walking out of the store, her arms laden down with bags.

"I could put a bag over my head and Rigid would still tell me I'm the sexiest woman. It gets annoying."

We all looked at Cyn like she was insane. What the hell was she talking about? I would love to have a man who would think I am sexy no matter what. "What the hell are you talking about?"

"Yeah, girl. I think we need to check your temperature or something."

"Ugh, I didn't mean it like that. It's just... oh shit, I don't even know what I'm saying. I've become such a bitch since I've become pregnant. It will be a miracle if Rigid is still with me by the time I pop this baby out."

"Oh, Cyn. It's just hormones, honey. I went through it when I had Remy. One minute I was a raging bitch, and then the next I was sweet as pie. You just need to realize when you're a complete bitch and just reel it in. Rigid is not going to leave you. That man is so in love with you he'd die before he left you." Meg wrapped her arm around Cyn's shoulders and pulled her into a hug.

"I'm sorry, guys. I've really ruined our shopping trip," Cyn cried.

"Oh shit, here comes the waterworks," Marley mumbled next to me. Right on cue, Cyn burst into tears, blubbering all over Meg's shoulder.

"Remind me never to get pregnant. I don't think Troy could handle the hormones or the tears."

"As long as you remind me of the same thing," I smirked. Marley held her hand out to me, and we shook on it.

"Oh Jesus, Gambler is wearing off on you if you two just made a bet," Demon said, walking up to us. He stood next to Marley and me, watching Meg and Cyn.

"No bet. Just agreeing to remind each other of the wonders of being pregnant," Marley said, motioning to Cyn.

"What the hell is wrong?" Rigid thundered, pushing past us. He pulled Cyn out of Meg's arms and wrapped himself around her.

"I'm so... so... sorry," Cyn hiccupped. "I'm such a bitch to you," she wailed.

Rigid rubbed her back, whispering to her. I turned away, not able to watch because I was so jealous that Cyn had such a wonderful man. Don't get me wrong, I was happy she had that, but it just made me realize that I didn't have that.

"Oh jeez, Rigid told me about this," King said, walking up with a Sears bag in one hand and an enormous pretzel in the other. He stood next to me, giving me the play by play of what was going on.

"Ugh, she just wiped her nose on his sleeve," he said, cringing. "Oh jeez, Meg's searching for something in her purse. Lord knows what she's going to pull out of there. Could be a fucking stuffed penguin for all I know. Last night I asked her for a pen and it took her ten minutes to find one. Although, in the search for the pen, she found three check stubs, five packs of gum, ten fruit snacks, an old romance novel, and twenty-three green Skittles."

"Twenty-three green Skittles?" Who the hell has only green Skittles in their purse?

"Yup," King took a huge bite of the pretzel and laughed. "Not a fucking clue why they were all green either. She was just as surprised as I was. She said it was probably

Troy the last time they went to the movies. They're always doing stupid shit to each other."

Well, I guess that made sense, sort of. "Did she ever find a pen?"

"Yeah, a green one," King burst out laughing.

"He told you about the Skittles, didn't he?" Meg asked walking over to King.

"Babe, it was fucking hilarious. Even you were shocked when you found the Skittles."

Meg grabbed the pretzel from him and tore a piece off and shoved it in her mouth, mumbling about Troy.

"Yo, I just got a text from Roam. He said they should be back to the clubhouse in forty-five minutes," Demon said, his phone in hand.

My ears perked up at the mention of Roam, knowing that Gambler was with him.

"Alright, you ready to head back, babe?" King asked, wrapping his arm around Meg.

"I wanted to hit up Torrid yet. I promise it'll only take ten minutes. Scouts honor." Meg held her hand up with the pretzel in it, salt falling to the floor.

"I know how you are shopping. Ten minutes turns into an hour and three more stores."

"We already hit up all the other stores I wanted to go to. Torrid and then we can go home, and I'll show you what I just bought." Meg leaned into King, trailing a finger down his shirt. She licked her lips and winked.

King was a goner as soon as she licked her lips. He wrapped both arms around her and kissed the hell out of her. She dropped the pretzel as she delved her fingers into his hair and held on.

"Jesus Christ. Get a fucking room," Demon grumbled, shoving his phone back in his pocket. King reached out, putting his hand on Demon's face and pushed him away.

"What the fuck?" he growled.

"Mind your own fucking business, brother," King mumbled, pulling away from Meg.

"Five minutes, tops," Meg breathed out, holding five fingers up.

"Five minutes for what?" Rigid asked, walking over with Cyn under his arm. Her eyes were red and puffy, but she had, at least, stopped crying.

"Meg promised King we would only spend five minutes in Torrid," Marley explained, pulling her phone out of her purse.

"Yeah, well, she promised that, not me," Cyn sassed, her hands propped on her hips.

"I'm with Cyn," I said, lacing my arm through hers.

"I'm good with whatever," Marley said, shoving her phone back in her pocket. "Troy isn't going to be back to the clubhouse for at least an hour."

"You've been overruled, King. Five minutes is barely enough time to make it past the sales tables." Cyn smirked.

King's eyes traveled over all of us, scowling. "Meg."

Meg shrugged her shoulders and held her hands up. "Hey, who am I to argue?" Meg glanced at Cyn and winked.

"Just one time I'd like a day where I don't have to deal with your crazy ass."

"Maybe one day, but today is not that day," Meg laughed, grabbing Cyn's other arm and pulled us in the direction of Torrid. "Give me half an hour and I'll give you an answer to the question you asked me before," Meg called over her shoulder.

"Oh my fucking God! You still haven't answered him?" Cyn said, her jaw dropped open.

"We were busy with kidnappings and houses blowing up. Me marrying Lo wasn't high on my priority list," Meg muttered.

Holy shit! Meg and King were going to get married! How fucking awesome! "Do you have a date set yet?"

"Pfft, first I need to say yes."

Cyn yanked on Meg's arm, stopping her in her tracks. "Your ass better say yes."

"I have no idea what my ass is going to say. But I'm pretty sure my mouth is going to say yes."

Cyn squealed and raised her arms up in the air, tossing up devil horns. "Fuck yes! I so get to be your maid of honor!"

"You're gonna have to be co-maid of honor with Mel."

Cyn pouted but nodded her head yes. "I'm good with that. Your sister is pretty cool."

"I'm glad you approve. Now let's get a move on." Meg grabbed Cyn's arm again and we continued to the store.

"Wait for me, bitches!" Marley yelled from behind us. I looked over my shoulder to see Marley sprinting to catch up with us, her long blonde hair flowing behind her. She threaded her arm through mine, and we were walking four wide down the mall. I'm pretty sure no one could get past us if they wanted.

"What the hell was all the squealing about?" Marley asked.

"Meg's going to marry King."

"It's about time he puts a ring on it," Cyn mumbled.

"We haven't even been together for a year."

"Yeah, well, it doesn't matter how long you two have been together. You're a match made in heaven with that man." Cyn opened her purse and pulled out a pack of gum, offering us each a piece.

I grabbed one and popped it into my mouth as I looked behind us, King, Rigid, and Demon trailing about twenty feet away. Three gorgeous men and none of them were mine. Not that I wanted any of them, but it would have been nice to have Gambler here.

I turned back around and sighed. Ugh, it was partly my fault why Gambler wasn't here. I should have pulled my head out of my ass and told the man what I wanted. Now I had pissed him off with all my nagging.

Oy. It was time to do some fixing. I already had a plan working in my head that included my new purchases at Victoria's Secret. Maybe I could find something to top off my plan to make Gambler mine.

All my cards were on the table. It was time to go all in on Gambler.

''*'*'*'*'*'*'*'*'*'*'*'*

Chapter 19

GAMBLER

Two fucking hours later and we were finally pulling up to the clubhouse. I swear to Christ Slider and Roam were trying to keep me away from the clubhouse. We had ended up stopping at two gas stations because when we stopped for Roam the first time, Slider didn't need gas but then forty-five minutes later we needed to stop for him and then he decided he was hungry so we ate at the fucking diner that was connected.

Longest two fucking hours of my life.

I glanced around the parking lot, seeing Gwen's little Beetle and all the other girl's cars were there, too.

I had no idea what the fuck I was going to do, but I had to do something. I couldn't go on with Gwen driving me crazy and not finding any release.

I turned back to the clubhouse to see Turtle walking out the door, lighting a cigarette. "It's about time ya'll got back. Meg's in the kitchen cooking dinner, trying to teach Marley how to not burn water and Cyn and Gwen are challenging all the guys to a pool tournament. I do have to say, that Gwen sure does have some fine assets." Turtle winked and took a long drag.

What the fuck did he just say? Here I was worrying about Demon and come to find out I have to worry about the whole fucking club possibly going after Gwen. I swung my leg over my bike and stalked to the door.

"Yo! Calm down, Gambler!" I heard Roam call, but I didn't fucking listen. The only way I was going to get these fuckers to lay off Gwen was to fucking take what was mine.

I swung open the door and saw red when my eyes connected with Gwen's ass that was pointed at the fucking door as she bent over the pool table lining up her shot. She was wearing skin tight pants and sky-high heels that made my blood boil and made me want to rip all her clothes off and fuck her in just the heels.

All eyes were on her as she wiggled her ass and took her shot. I could only imagine what she looked like from the front laid out on the pool table. She drove me crazy in her see through tank tops and short shorts at night. All of those nights didn't compare to this moment right now. Fully clothed and covered, she drove me absolutely insane.

She jumped up from the table, arms in the air after she made the shot and spun around. An enormous grin on her face until her eyes connected with mine. The color drained from her face, and I could tell she was surprised to see me.

She took a step towards me, and I shook my head no. I stalked toward her, my eyes only on her. Everyone else in the club faded away.

"I didn't know if-" she started to ramble but stopped when I stooped down, put my shoulder in her stomach and lifted her up. I didn't miss a step as I tossed her over my shoulder and headed toward the hallway.

"Dinner will be done in half an hour ya'll," Meg said, walking out of the kitchen and right into me.

"Save us a plate. We're gonna be a while," I mumbled, walking around her.

"Oh shit, it's about to go down," Meg said in awe. "Don't come out until ya'll know what the hell you two are!" she hollered at my retreating back.

"Gambler?"

I didn't say anything. I had no idea what to say to Gwen right now that wouldn't make me sound like some caveman. All I wanted to do was pound on my chest and scream mine.

"Are you mad at me?"

I grabbed my keys out of my pocket and unlocked my door. I flipped the light switch on and tossed Gwen on the bed.

"What the hell do you think you're doing?" she demanded as she bounced on the bed, her hair falling in her face.

"I don't have a fucking clue what I'm doing anymore, Gwen! You're driving me fucking crazy!" I ran my fingers through my hair and paced in front of the bed.

"Me?! What about you? This morning you blow up at me and roar off on your bike and now come back and carry me off like some caveman, and I'm just supposed to be OK with this? You're confusing the shit out of me!" she wailed, rolling off the bed and getting in my face.

"I don't know what the hell you want!"

"Like I know what you want?"

"I come back from visiting my dead sister's grave and find you spread out on the fucking pool table putting on a God damn show!" I roared.

"How the hell was I supposed to know that was where you went? And, I wasn't spread out on the pool table! I was playing pool!" Her eyes flared with annoyance and she poked her finger into my chest.

"You better think twice before you do that again, doll," I warned, grabbing her hand.

"Oh yeah, what the hell are you going to do about it? Drive off and leave me all alone again?"

"I didn't leave you alone. I needed to clear my fucking head."

"Well, fucking tell me that! You left here, and I thought I did something wrong." She crossed her arms over her chest and glared at me.

"You fucking did! I can't get you out of my fucking head! You brush up against me, fawn over me, and don't even get me started how you wrap yourself around me when you sleep. I fucking need you and I can't God damn have you!"

"Who the hell says you can't have me?"

"Me! I know you're going to fucking destroy me. Something will happen and you'll be gone, and then I'll be right back where I was when I lost Evie. I can't fucking love someone and lose them again."

Gwen gasped and her eyes widened. "Who was Evie?" she whispered.

"My sister. I loved her and she died. She was the last person I loved besides my mom. I can't give that to someone again, Gwen, and you deserve more than what I can fucking give you."

"Don't you think I should be the fucking judge of what I deserve?"

"You don't know what you're asking for, Gwen. I see the way you watch King, Rigid, and Troy with the girls. I know you want that, and I don't think I can give that to you."

"Don't tell me what I fucking want! I want you, and I don't care if you think I deserve someone else!"

"You don't know what you are asking for," I growled. I was at the end of my patience with her. I could only warn her and fight with her so much.

"Give me what I want!"

"Don't push me, Gwen."

She stepped closer, her head tilted back a bit. Even with heels on I was still taller than her. "Take it, Gambler. Take me."

I couldn't do it anymore. I couldn't deny myself the one thing I needed and wanted. I grabbed her around the waist and spun her around, slamming her against the door. "This makes you mine, Gwen. There's no going back." This was her last chance to change her mind.

"I've never wanted anything more in my life," she whispered.

I slammed my mouth down on her's and groaned as she instantly opened, yielding to me. My hands immediately went to her ass, lifting her up. She wrapped her legs around my waist, her heels digging into my back. "I wanna fuck you with just the heels on," I growled.

She wrapped her legs around me tighter and tossed her head back as I trailed kisses down her neck, tasting what I had been craving.

I reached up, grabbing one side of her shirt and ripped it open. She gasped in surprise but didn't stop me as I pulled her bra down and devoured her perfect tit. "Gambler," she moaned, arching her body into me.

She tugged at her shirt, twisting out of it and tossed it on the floor. I reached behind her, trying to free her perfect tits and moaned as her bra hit the floor. "You're not allowed to ever put clothes on again."

A laugh bubbled out of her and she cradled my face in her hands. "That sounds good now, but I'm pretty sure the first one of your friends to see me naked will end up dead."

"You're probably right. I'll just have to keep you in my room and never let you out."

"Now that has promise," she said, nibbling on my bottom lip.

"Don't tempt me, doll. Slide down, we both have too many clothes on right now for this to go the way I want."

"So demanding," she purred unwrapping her legs from me. Her feet touched the floor, but she kept her arms wrapped around my neck. "Everything off but the heels?"

"Heels stay, the rest better be off in ten seconds." I pulled my coat and cut off, turning around and tossed them on the bed. I turned back around, tugging my shirt over my head to see Gwen hopping from foot to foot pulling her pants off. I glimpsed a tiny purple triangle of cloth covering her sweet pussy, and I swear I could have cum in my jeans right there.

I watched as she struggled to pull her pants over the heels. Her pants were skin tight and there was no way she was going to get them off. "Stop," I said, kneeling down in from of her. I grabbed her right foot, slipping her heel off and then her pant leg. I did the same with the left and then put both heels back on.

"What about my panties?" she asked as I stood up.

"They stay on for now." I unbuttoned my jeans, watching as she bit her bottom lip. I leaned down, quickly unlacing my boots and kicked them off. Her tongue snaked out, licking her lips as I tugged my jeans down, my underwear coming down with them. "This first time is going to go fast, doll. I've wanted you for over a month. I'm pretty sure my dick is going to explode when it feels your tight pussy." I pulled my pants down the rest of the way, my dick rock hard and bobbing.

Gwen took a step towards me, her hand reaching out. "No." She stopped in her tracks, confusion crossing her face. "Turn around, brace your hands on the door," I ordered.

She hesitantly turned around, her eyes not leaving mine until she was entirely turned around. "I want to touch you, Gambler. Please," she begged as she put her hands on the door.

"I told you I'm on the edge, doll. One touch from you and this is going to be over before we even start." I stepped forward and trailed a finger down the center of her back. "So smooth," I murmured.

Her body shivered under my touch, a moan escaping from her lips. Her head fell forward and her back arched. "You're torturing me," she whispered.

"Now you know how I've felt every night you wrapped your sweet, soft body around me." I wrapped my arms around her and pulled her to me. "Spread your legs, doll." She shuffled her feet a couple of inches apart and waited. Her breathing was shallow and short, and I knew she needed this just as much as I did.

I reached around and cupped her pussy, her lips drenched with her desire. "So wet for me," I murmured as I parted her slick lips. She trembled in my arms, and I placed my other hand on her stomach. My dick was cradled in the crack of her ass and it took all my self-control not to bend her over and plow into her. "I'm going to make you come all over my hand," I whispered, "and then you're going to come even harder around my dick."

A tremor rocked through her body and she tossed her head back, exposing her neck to me. I slipped a finger inside her as I trailed kisses down her neck.

"Gambler," she moaned as I pumped my finger in and out. I added another finger and her tight pussy pulsed around them, making my dick rock hard and beg to be buried inside her. I flicked her clit with my thumb, her pussy drenched with her desire.

"Are you gonna cum for me, doll?" I growled in her ear.

"Yes," she hissed as I worked her clit, bringing her closer and closer to the edge. She threw her arms over her head and wrapped them around my head and held on. "I'm so close."

She arched her back, pressing her sweet ass into my rock hard dick. She rocked her body with the thrusting of my fingers, moans, and mewls of pleasure gasping from her lips.

"Cum for me, Gwen. Now," I demanded as I bit down on her ear lobe. I pinched her clit, and she exploded around my fingers, her screams of ecstasy surrounding me. Her body bucking with every wave of pleasure that washed over her.

"Gambler," she moaned as her body came down, small tremors still taking over her body. She leaned back into me, the full weight of her pressed against me. "Holy fuck," she cursed, resting her head on my shoulder.

"That was the sexiest thing I've ever seen," I growled, kissing her neck.

"Hmm it sure felt good," she purred.

"Are you OK to stand?" I asked, trailing my hands up her body and cupped her perfect tits.

"As long as you hold me up," she laughed.

"Hmm, I had plans of bending you over right here."

"Jesus Christ," she gasped as another tremor rocked through her body. "Just the thought of you bending me over could make me cum."

"How about my dick makes you cum next, doll. Next time we can see if you can cum from just my voice." I stepped back, holding onto her arms making sure she was steady enough to stand. "You good, doll?"

She nodded her head and looked over her shoulder at me. "Never better."

I put my hand on the small of her back and slowly pushed her down till she was bent over, her ass in the air. "I've dreamed of seeing you like this. Bent over, ready and waiting for me," I murmured, running my hand over the fullness of her ass.

"Take me, Gambler," she begged.

I stroked my cock as I caressed her ass, spreading her cheeks, seeing her dripping wet pussy waiting for me. I stepped forward, my dick nudging the tight rose of her ass. She gasped, a slow moan escaping her lips as I trailed my dick down the crack of her ass and lined my dick up with her sweet pussy.

I slammed into her, unable to take things slow any longer. "Hold onto your ankles, baby." I watched as her hands slid down her legs, and she wrapped her fingers around her delicate ankles. I rocked slowly in and out of her, eager to fuck the shit out of her, but not wanting it to be over that quickly.

"Harder," she moaned.

"I go harder and I'll be done in ten seconds," I gritted out.

"Not to freak you out, but you don't have a condom on." Holy fuck! I pulled out but was stopped when Gwen reached, holding my legs so I couldn't pull out all the way. "I'm on the pill, and there is no way we are going to use a condom after I felt how perfect you fit inside me."

"Jesus fucking Christ, Gwen. How the hell am I supposed to stop after you said that?"

"You're not. That's exactly why I said it. If you stop, I'll kill you," she threatened. She dug her nails into my leg, tightening her grip.

I slowly sunk back into her as she tossed her head back. "Fuck," I moaned as she squeezed the walls of her pussy around my dick.

"Fuck me hard, Gambler. Make it better than anything I've ever felt."

She didn't have to tell me twice. "Can you reach down and put your hands on the floor?" She reached down without a word, but we both moaned as she leaned forward, and I slipped even further into her. "Hold on, doll. I'm gonna fuck the shit out of you."

I pulled out and slammed back into her, her body rocking forward. She braced her hands farther apart and waited for more. I slowly slid out, leaving only the tip inside her. She rocked her body backward and slammed down on my dick. "Fuck me, Gambler. I don't want gentle. I want everything you can give me."

I growled at her words, wondering how the hell I had gotten so lucky to find this perfect woman. I grabbed her waist, my fingertips digging into her hips and slammed into her, the tight walls of her pussy contracting around me. I thrust in and out, each one better than the last.

"Yes," she moaned, as I pounded into her, reaching for my release. I reached around, parted the lips of her pussy and flicked her clit. "Gambler," she screamed. She stumbled forward as her orgasm crashed into her, but I caught her by her hips as I slammed into her one last time as I came in her tight, sweet pussy that was milking every last drop of cum from me. "Holy fuck," I groaned, throwing my head back. I leaned forward, covering her body with mine, and lifted her up, helping her stand up.

Her head limply laid on my shoulder, her breathing labored and short. "I have no idea what that position was called but we need to do that again. Soon."

"First I need to sit down before I fall down, doll." I leaned over, lifting her into my arms and turned around and laid her on the bed. She scooted up to the pillows and pulled the covers back. She slipped under them and held the sheet back, waiting for me.

"You do know it's only four o'clock, right?"

She shrugged her shoulders and patted the mattress. "Who said anything about sleeping?"

''*'*'*'*'*'*'*'*'*

Chapter 20

Gwen

I was beyond exhausted, but I wanted more. I don't think I would ever get tired of this man. Gambler looked down at me, smirking and my heart melted a little bit. That fucking smirk drove me crazy. I grabbed his arm and tugged him down on the mattress.

He crawled on top of me, caging me in with his arms and trapping me with his body. "You're just a little vixen, aren't you, doll?"

"Only for you," I purred, reaching up, stroking his cheek. He had a weeks' worth of stubble, and it drove me mad. Each day he became more and more gorgeous. "I like this," I murmured.

He leaned his cheek into my hand, "Maybe I'll keep it for a while since you seem to be a fan of it."

"I wonder what it would feel like everywhere."

Gambler leaned down, rubbing his cheek against the side of my breast. "You mean here?" he mumbled.

The scratchy roughness drove me crazy as he worked his way down my stomach, raining kisses as he went. "Hmm, maybe just a little lower," I cooed.

"Here?" He nipped at my side.

"Closer."

He kneeled in between my legs, spreading them wide. "Right here?" he whispered, a breath away from my core. I dug my fingers into the bed and nodded my head. "I need to hear you, doll. Tell me where you want it."

"Make me cum," I pleaded, arching my back.

"Hmm, I've already done that twice." He parted the lips of my pussy, his breath teasing me. "How should I make you come?"

Oh my God. Just his voice was setting me on the brink of coming. One touch from him and I knew I was going to go off like a rocket. "Your tongue. I need your tongue," I pleaded. He flicked my clit with the tip of his tongue and a tremor rocked my body.

"Like that?" I looked down my body to see Gambler smirking at me, his eyes burning with desire.

"More. I need more," I panted.

"Whatever you want, doll. It's all yours." His head disappeared, and he sucked my clit into his mouth, his tongue swirling, and kneading.

I dug my heels into the bed, lifting my body up, reaching for more. Gambler put his hand on my stomach, pushing me down back on the bed. His hand glided up, grabbing my breast, pinching the nipple in between his fingers. I was in fucking heaven and hell all at the same time. I had never felt the way Gambler made me feel before, but it was pure torture, and I wanted more.

Gambler looked up, his eyes connecting with mine. I bit my lip as I caught a glimpse of his tongue flicking my clit. "Fuck me," he groaned, raising his head. "I bet your fucking mouth was made for my dick." He grabbed my hand, pulling me up and rolled us over so I was sprawled out on top of him.

"Hmm, I liked what you were doing," I pouted, kissing his neck.

He grabbed my ass, "Flip around, doll, I want you sucking my cock while I eat that sweet pussy." He smacked my ass and pressed a kiss to my forehead.

I moaned as I slid down his body and swung my leg over his body and came face to face with his rock hard dick. He didn't need to tell me twice to do anything. Everything he wanted was the same thing I needed. I slid his cock into my mouth, moaning as he spread the lips of my pussy and flicked my clit with his finger. "So wet," he mumbled. His tongue swirled around my clit, and I dug my nails into his thighs, holding on as he brought me to the edge with one touch. I bobbed my head up and down, my tongue feeling every ridge and vein of his cock.

Gambler grabbed my ass, pulling me down and buried his face in my pussy, licking and devouring every inch. "I'm gonna cum," I moaned, raising my head and stroked him with my hand.

"Mouth," Gambler muffled, slapping my ass.

I slid him back into my mouth as my hand stroked his shaft. I swirled my tongue around the tip and sucked hard as I moved my hand faster. I heard Gambler moan and knew he was just as close as I was. "Faster," he panted. "I want to cum down your throat while you scream my name."

There he goes again making me want to come from just his voice. I slide all the way down until he hit the back of my throat and swallowed. Gambler roared, his balls tightening and his dick pulsed under my tongue. He nipped at my clit and tipped me over the edge, my orgasm slamming into me as his cum coated my throat.

His fingers dug into my ass as he thrust into my mouth wringing every last drop of cum from him. My arms shook as I tried to hold myself, my orgasm rocking my body harder than the last time.

"God dammit, you are unbelievable."

I swirled my tongue one last time around the head of his dick, making sure not to miss a drop of his sweet cum and laid my head on his thigh. "No, I think you're the amazing one for making me cum three times in less than an hour."

He stroked my back, trailing his fingers in lazy circles. "Happy to be of service," he laughed, his body shaking under me.

I rolled off and face planted in the mattress, completely rung out. "You do know I'll be needing daily service from now on."

Gambler laughed even harder and sat up. He reached for me, grabbing my arms and pulled me into his lap. He brushed the hair out of my face and stroked my cheek. "Only is you promise to service me."

"I'm sure that can be arranged," I leaned up, my lips brushing against him. "I think you might have broken me for the rest of the night, though."

"I doubt that. I say we rest, get some dinner, and then maybe I can do some more service. You do know I'm a mechanic, so I like to be very thorough in my work. Check under the hood," he trailed his tongue between my breasts, "check the spark plus," his tongue snaked out, swirling around my nipple, "and you can't forget about checking the undercarriage." His hand cupped my pussy and another tremor of anticipation ran through me. How the hell did this man manage to make me cum three times and still leave me wanting more?

"I guess I better rest and prepare for my full inspection." I rested my head on his chest, the steady beating of his heart calming and lulling me to sleep.

I finally gave in to what I wanted and the world didn't end. Maybe I would get my happy ending after all.

''*'*'*'*'*'*'*'*'*'*'*'*

Chapter 21

GAMBLER

"Salsa?" Gwen asked, sitting back down in my lap as she poured a shit ton of salsa on her nachos.

After we had recovered by taking an hour nap, we managed to find our clothes we had tossed all over the room and ventured out to the kitchen. Meg was just about to put a plate up for us as we walked in.

We both piled our plates high and headed over to the table where Roam, Hammer, Slider, and King were playing poker. "Go get another chair," King said to Hammer as we set our plates down.

"No, we're good," Gwen said, waving her hand at Ham to sit down.

"Doll, where the hell are you going to sit?"

"On you."

Which lead us to now. She perched on my knee and shoveled a forkful into her mouth.

"How they hell do you eat so much?" Ham asked, his eyes following Gwen's every move.

Roam slapped him upside the head and scoffed, "Don't you have any common sense?" he asked.

"What the hell was that for?" he asked, rubbing his head. "I just wanted to know how she had such a smokin' body when she eats like a God damn truck driver. That's her third plate."

Gwen laughed next to me and took a swig of the margarita Meg had handed to her when we walked out of the kitchen. Meg had been up twice to fill her glass up. Apparently it was a bottomless margarita. "Gambler worked up my appetite." She winked at me as she piled more food on her fork.

"Alright, I'm done. Next time I make tacos someone else is doing the dishes. I make too big of a mess to clean up myself," Meg laughed, carrying the big pitcher of margaritas in one hand and her glass in the other. She set it in front of Gwen and plopped down in King's lap.

"I would have helped you," Gwen said, shoveling the last of her food in her mouth. I really must have worked her appetite up. I was on my second plate, and I was full.

"Eh, that was more directed at Lo than you," Meg laughed, taking a drink.

"I told you what needed to happen before I'd do the dishes." King set his cards down and wrapped his arms around Meg. "All I need to hear is one little word out of that pretty little mouth."

Meg rolled her eyes but didn't say anything. "Dude, you promised you would answer him if he let you go in Torrid today. Never mind the fact that we almost spent an hour in there. Answer the man!" Cyn yelled from the couch. Rigid was sitting in the corner of the couch and Cyn was laying down, her head in his lap as he rubbed her stomach.

"You're not helping!" Meg yelled. "I thought you were supposed to be my ride or die bitch. Now you're just throwing me to the wolves."

"King is far from a wolf," Cyn countered.

"They do realize you're sitting right here?" I asked King.

He just shrugged his shoulders and picked up his cards. "I'm used to it. Cyn will probably get an answer out of her before I will." Meg grabbed his cards out of his hands and tossed them on the table. "Babe," he called as he watched his cards scatter and fall on the floor.

"Ask me again," she demanded.

"What?" King said.

"Ask me again. Do it."

"Meg, I don't want to do this if you're just going to say yes to make everyone else happy. I'm good with how we are. Forget I even asked." King lifted Meg off his lap and headed to the bar. I could tell he was either pissed off or disappointed. Either way, he wasn't in a good mood anymore.

Meg looked around, shocked. "You take it back?"

King picked up a bottle of Jim Beam and filled his glass. "I don't want to make you do something you don't want. I don't take it back, but I'm not going to hassle you about it anymore. When you're ready, let me know."

"But I am ready."

King shook his head and set his glass down. "If you were ready, babe, you would have already said yes."

I looked around the poker table and Roam, Ham, and Slider each looked like they wanted to slide under the table and disappear. Gwen was sitting next to me her jaw hanging open, looking at Meg and King. I had no idea what the hell was going on, but it was either going to end good or bad. Right now I would have betted on bad.

"I wanna say yes," Meg insisted, stomping her foot.

"No, ya don't. A man shouldn't have to ask a woman five times to marry him before he gets an answer. I love you, Meg, and I'm not going anywhere, but I can only take so much rejection before I get the point. Marriage is a no."

"But that's not what I want," she wailed, throwing her arms up in the air.

"Well, then fucking tell me what you want. I hear more from your friends of what you want than you!"

"God dammit, Lo! I fucking love you and you better believe your ass is going to marry me! I don't care what anyone else says or thinks. Stop listening to them, and listen to me!" Everyone went silent. Cyn and Rigid sat up from the couch and peered over the back of it.

Marley and Troy came walking down the hallway, but stopped in their tracks when they saw Meg and King squared off on each other.

"God dammit, Meg. This is what you want? In front of everybody?"

"I don't care who's in this room right now besides you. If you're here, it's what I want. I don't want anyone else." Tears were streaming down her face as she waited.

King ran his fingers through his hair, his eyes never leaving Meg. "I fucking love you. With everything I am and will be, I love you. I want to wake up every morning next to you in our big ass bed and every night I want you next to me in that big ass bed so we can do it all over again the next day. I love your son, I love your dog, but most of all I love you. Without you I'm nothing and with you I'm everything. Marry me?"

Meg nodded her head, her hand covering her mouth. Holy shit, King had some moves. He even had me wanting to say yes.

Gwen reached for her napkin and blotted her eyes. I pulled her hair out of my way and kissed her neck. "You OK, doll?"

She nodded her head and buried her face in my neck. "Meg deserves this," she mumbled.

I wrapped my arms tight around her and held her close.

"Is that a yes?" King asked.

Meg nodded her head again and sobbed. I glanced over at Troy and Marley, who both had huge grins plastered on their faces and Cyn was quietly crying as Rigid rubbed her back.

"It's about fucking time," King mumbled. He closed the distance between them and lifted her in her arms and swung her around.

"Well, I guess that's one way to get engaged," Roam said, taking a sip from his beer.

Gwen spit out the sip of margarita she took and busted out laughing. "What the hell, doll?" I asked, wiping off my hands she had just spat over.

"Roam is right. That really was a Meg way to get engaged. Holler and yell at each other and then get engaged," Cyn laughed.

"Oh shut up," Meg said, flipping the bird at all of us. "You all knew I was going to say yes," she scoffed.

King reached into his back pocket and pulled his wallet. "Good man, he knows as soon as she says yes to just hand his wallet over to her. Exhibit A of why the hell I will *never* get married." Slider wiped his mouth with the back of his palm and raised his glass up to Meg and King.

"I'm not giving her my fucking wallet," King grumbled as he searched through his wallet. "I knew that when she said yes, it was going to be in some crazy way. That's why I kept the ring in my pocket." King pulled it out and got down on one knee. "Megan Marie Grain, ever since you've come into my life, nothing has been the same. You're the reason I laugh and smile every day. Will you marry me?"

And, just like in true Meg fashion, she nodded her head yes and tackled him to the ground. "Yes, yes, yes a thousand times!" she yelled.

"Well, I didn't know we were going to get a show with our tacos," Gwen said, turning her head to look at me.

"Neither did I, doll," I brushed my lips against her's, craving her taste.

She threaded her fingers through my hair and pulled me close. "Last one to the bedroom is a rotten egg." She jumped up from my lap and sprinted down the hall without looking back.

"What the fuck?" Slider said, watching Gwen run away.

I shook my head and grabbed our empty plates and carried them to the kitchen. "Hey, where are you going?" Cyn called. "We need to celebrate!"

I shook my head and wiped my pants on my jeans. "I think Gwen has her own kind of celebration in mind," I called, raising my hand over my head and headed down the hall.

I rubbed my hands together hopeful that by the time I made it to our room, Gwen would have her clothes off and spread out on the bed for me.

Today had ended completely different from how it started. It had started out with Gwen and I ready to claw each other's eyes out and now all I wanted to do was rip her clothes off and bury myself in her for hours.

I turned the handle on the door and pushed it open. And to top the night off, Gwen was laid out on the bed wearing nothing but a smile and her high heels.

Let the celebration begin.

''*'*'*'*'*'*'*'*'*'*'*

Chapter 22

Gwen

"How many boxes can one woman have?" I groaned, lifting up another box from the trunk of Paige's car.

"I don't know, doll. She's your sister." Gambler grabbed the box from my arms and set it on top of the last one in the trunk and lifted them both.

"I could have taken that," I whined, slamming the lid shut.

"I know. Doesn't mean you have to." Gambler winked at me and head into the two bedroom Paige had found the day she arrived in town. It was two blocks away from my salon and over the pet store. Plus, our aunt lived only five minutes away, so it was perfect.

I glanced into the backseat of her car, double-checking to make sure we didn't miss anything and headed into the house. "I think that's it, Paige," I said, shutting the door behind me. It was two weeks away from Thanksgiving and there was a definite chill in the air. I pulled my cardigan tight around me and rubbed my hands together.

"You want these in the kitchen?" Gambler asked.

"Um, I'm not really sure what they are," Paige mumbled standing up from unpacking a box that was full of cow figurines. Yes, the whole collection of Mary Moo Moo's had made the move with Paige.

Gambler shook the box and it sounded like silverware rattling around. "I think I'll just set it in the kitchen," he mumbled.

Paige had gotten into town yesterday and it had been a whirlwind to say the least.

Before Paige arrived, Gambler and I spent most of our time in his room surfacing only to go to work and eat. I never thought that Gambler would be so demanding and dominate. I was falling quick and fast for the man I was terrified to love.

He anticipated all my needs and gave me everything I could ever want or need. I was in a blissful haze that I never wanted to leave.

A pounding on the door made me jump, "That must be Meg and Marley," I mumbled, opening the door.

Meg stood on the other side with King next to her. "Don't ask. Apparently shit has gone down and I'm not allowed to leave the clubhouse on my own." Meg rolled her eyes and walked into the small living room.

King followed Meg in, looking annoyed and ready to wring her neck. "I'm sorry me keeping you safe is inconvenient for you, babe."

"Ugh, I don't mean it, Lo. I'm a bitch today, apparently. I'm sick of having to look over my shoulder all the time and worrying if someone is going to get hurt again." Meg ran her fingers through her hair and sighed. I couldn't agree with her more. Every time Gambler would go to work I was terrified something would happen.

"As soon as Leo and his sister get here, things will change. He said they should be here this weekend and that he had some interesting information for us. We just need to make it two more days." King took his coat off and tossed it on the back of the couch. "Where's Gambler?"

I pointed to the kitchen and King headed that way. Meg sat down next to me and held her hand out to Paige. "I'm Meg. That big hunk in the kitchen is King, he belongs to me."

Paige shook her hand and laughed. "Good to know."

"He's also her fiancée," I chimed in, sitting on the couch.

Meg waved her hand at me, shushing me. "Ignore her."

"Oh, he's not your fiancée?" Paige asked, confused.

"He is, but I don't feel it necessary to tell everyone I meet like Gwen here does. I figure with me saying he belongs to me was good enough." Meg stuck her tongue out at me and flipped me off.

I was coming to realize if Meg flipped you off, it was her way of saying she liked you. Strange, but so Meg. "Is Marley coming?"

"Naw, her and Troy were cuddled up at the clubhouse watching TV. She said she'll get over to meet Paige the next couple of days."

Paige stood up and carried a box over to her bookshelf Gambler had put together earlier. "It's the cows!" Meg hollered as she watched Paige line them up on the shelf.

Paige laughed and shook her head. "I'm assuming Gwen informed you about my cows?"

"She sure did, and I had no idea what the hell she was talking about. I did ask Ethel and she knew what they were. I'm apparently out of the loop."

"Where has Ethel been?" I asked, grabbing the other box of cows and took them over to Paige.

"Somehow Gravel and her are able to stay at her house. King said he doesn't think they'll go after them. King takes me over there every couple days to keep me from going crazy being cooped up at the clubhouse. He either loves me, or he knows I'll cut him if he doesn't let me out," Meg laughed.

"The answer is a little bit of both, babe." King and Gambler walked back into the living room, both looking at what Paige was doing. They both apparently had never seen a Mary Moo Moo before. I had grown up with them, so I didn't think they were strange at all.

"I gotta make a couple of phone calls, babe. You good in here with your girls?" King asked, pulling his phone out of his pocket.

"Go, shoo. We'll holler if we need anything. Like pizza or wine," Meg said, waving her hand at him. King leaned down, pressing a kiss to the side of her head and walked out the door.

"I'll be right outside, doll." Gambler wrapped his arms around me and kissed me like he hadn't seen me in years.

I grabbed his biceps and held on. It was the only thing I could do when Gambler kissed me. The man knew what he was doing with his mouth.

He pulled back, a smirk playing on his lips. "Miss me," he winked and walked out the door.

"Holy hell," Meg said, her jaw dropped. "I think Gambler just made me swoon." She fanned herself with her hand and pulled her shirt away trying to get air under it.

"For the record, even though you are my sister, that was pretty freakin' hot." Paige set her empty box on the floor and took the one I was holding out of my hands.

"When I finally let myself be with Gambler, I never imagined he would be the way he is." I grabbed another box and opened it seeing more cows. I now knew that when I wondered how the hell Paige could have so much stuff, I realized half the boxes were filled with cows.

"Oh, do tell how Gambler is." Meg grabbed a pillow off the couch and stuffed it under her head and laid down.

"I thought you came here to help unpack?" I asked.

"I'd much rather hear how Gambler is than put shit away. No offense, Paige."

Paige laughed and shook her head. "I'm not worried. I don't need everything put away right away. I can't tell you the last time I just hung out and chilled with friends. We can talk, and I can organize my cows."

"I think we might have to get you a new hobby."

"It's useless, Meg. Paige and my aunt have been obsessed with these damn cows since they came out." I grabbed another box off the floor and wasn't surprised to see it stuffed full with more cows.

"You mean to tell me you're not down with the cows?" Meg laughed. "Although you two really don't look anything alike. Paige is all sexy, sweet, innocence while you're sexy pinup. The only way I can tell you two are related is your eyes."

"Muddy brown," Paige and I said at the same time. We both hated our eye color.

"Dude," Meg said, sitting up. "Your eyes are like dark pools of chocolate. Or that could be my hunger talking." Meg scratched her head and laughed. "But anyway, your eyes rock."

Paige and I both laughed. "You are right that we are nothing alike. Except when we were growing up, Gwen *always* tried to dress like me. That is until she met Matt Crown and everything changed."

"Shut up," I yelled, grabbing a pillow off the couch and threw it at her.

"Hey, watch the cows," she whined, throwing her body in front of the bookcase.

"No one wants to hear about Matt." I crossed my arms over my chest and glared at Paige. I hadn't thought about Matt in ages, and I didn't want to start now.

"Matthew Crown was the first ever to turn Gwen's head and she was stuck on him for years. I'm talking six years, here."

"Wow, six years. When did you two meet?"

"Oh my God, I can't believe we are talking about this. I totally regret talking you into moving up here. Pack all this shit up and go."

"Oh, hush, woman," Paige threw her empty box on the floor and took the full from one my hands. "She was fifteen when she met him. He moved in next door to us and Gwen was totally smitten."

"Who the hell says smitten?" I mumbled, collapsing on the floor next to Meg.

"I do. Now shut up. If you don't want to tell the story, then I will."

"It's all lies," I said, looking at Meg.

Meg just shook her head and wrapped her arms around my shoulders. "Hush, it's story time." She put her finger over my mouth and winked.

"Sooo, back to what I was saying. Matt was the complete and total bad boy. He was two years older than Gwen and, in my opinion, was a complete and total ass. Drop dead gorgeous, but still an ass."

"Ugh, they totally lose points when they're asses," Meg agreed.

"Now our Gwen was nothing to scoff about. Even when I was eighteen and she was fifteen, her boobs were bigger than mine. Matt took one look at both of us and also became totally smitten with Gwen."

"There's that fucking word again," I muttered.

Paige rolled her eyes but kept going. "I'm not all sure what happened because I did move away from home, but things were going pretty good for these two until one night Matt went to a party by himself and had a little bit too much to drink. At this point, they were five years into their love/infatuation and Gwen thought rainbows and ponies shot out of Matt's ass. I knew better."

"You did not. Nobody expected it to happen."

"I saw it coming. I couldn't pinpoint exactly what was about to happen, but I knew."

"Holy freakin' shit! Would one of you please tell me what the hell happened!" Meg gripped my arm, anxiously waiting.

It was a definite dousey what happened. Paige could say it till she was blue in the face that she knew, but I doubt she did. Even Matt's own mom didn't know. "Matt was gay."

"What!?!? You dated a gay guy for six years! Wait, you said after five years you found out. You stayed with him even when you knew he was gay?"

"She sure did. Matt was too much of a chicken to come out of the closet. He begged and pleaded with Gwen to stay with him."

"Wait, hold the fucking gay train up a minute here. Did you have sex with him before all this came out?" Meg turned to me, her eyes bulging out of her head.

"Um, yeah."

"So how the hell did he have sex with you? Was he like bi or something? How the hell did he get hard?" Meg lifted her pinkie finger and wiggled it.

"I found out he had a good imagination," I winced, closing my eyes. Ugh, telling people about my sham of a relationship was not the shining moment of my life I wanted to talk about.

Hi, my name is Gwen, and I was so blind that I couldn't see that the man I was sleeping with every night was secretly picturing The Rock every time we had sex. Nope, not what I want people to know.

"Can we please stop talking about this? I was a fool and an idiot and trust me, I learned from it."

Paige sat down next to me and put her arm around my shoulder. "Nobody thinks you're a fool, hun. We all think Matt was an ass for lying to you for so long."

"Hell yeah, how the hell were you supposed to know he preferred salami to tuna?"

Paige and I burst out laughing, tears streaming down our faces.

"I thought you girls were unpacking?" I looked up and saw Gambler and King walk through the door.

"We were, but then we had to take a trip down memory lane about Gw-." I elbowed Paige to shut her up.

"We were just talking and Meg made a joke," I said, as Paige glared at me while she rubbed her side. I did not need Gambler knowing about my six-year mistake.

Imagine thinking you've found the man of your dreams, at fifteen no less, and then you decide to surprise him by showing up at a party and find him making out with a guy. Talk about a shock. Then I was an even bigger fool for staying with him for another year. We were both shocked when I walked in that room on him. Matt swore that was the first time he had kissed another guy. He insisted that he had too much to drink and one thing led to another. I could only imagine what would have happened if I hadn't walked in when I did.

He still called me a couple times of year to check up on me. I know he felt guilty for doing what he did to me and that was his way to make himself feel better. I always answered the phone when he called, but I never called him.

"What was the joke?" Gambler asked, sitting down on the couch.

Paige, Meg and I looked back and forth, scrambling for a joke.

"Uh, well, you know..." Paige trailed off, her hands held out in front of her.

"And then it, um, you know..." I wasn't much better at thinking on the spot.

"Pig fell in the mud!" Meg yelled. We all looked at her like she was crazy and her face turned bright red. "It was a dirty joke," she said, shrugging her shoulders.

Paige snorted and burst out laughing while King and Gambler rolled their eyes. "I feel like this is the whole drunk Marley and the coffee pot in the bathroom again. When am I going to learn that I can't leave you alone for that long?" King walked over to her and held his hand out. She grabbed on and he pulled her up and wrapped his arms around her. "What am I going to do with you?" he whispered. Meg wrapped her arms around his neck and whispered something in his ear. I could only imagine what came out of Meg's mouth.

"Watch this," Gambler said, nudging me with his foot and pointed to King and Meg. "Five, four, three, two, one," he mouthed.

"Well, it's time to get the fuck out of here," King boomed, grabbing Meg's hand and pulling her to the door.

"But I didn't help unpack anything," Meg laughed.

"You can come back tomorrow if I'm done with you by then."

"Oh, well, bye girls!" Meg waved as King pushed her out the door, waved to Gambler and slammed the door shut behind him.

"How the hell did you know that was going to happen?" I asked, standing up.

"Cause I heard what she was whispering to him."

"What did she say?" I mean, I could take a guess at what she said, but I wanted to know what Gambler heard. It probably had something to do with salami and tuna if I knew Meg.

"I'll show you when we get back to our room." Gambler reached forward, snagging my hand and pulled me into his lap.

I slapped his hand away as he traveled up my leg and laughed. "No, none of that right now. I need to help Paige. Our only other help just left, so now it's all on us."

"Um, I'm gonna order pizza," Paige mumbled, walking into the kitchen.

"Now you just embarrassed my sister," I scolded, hitting him in the chest.

Gambler grabbed my hand and pressed a kiss to my palm. "It's not my fault I can't keep my hands off you." He buried his face in my hair and rubbed my back.

I leaned into him, missing his touch. It was crazy how much I missed him when he had been within shouting distance of me. "I think I'm going crazy, Gambler."

"Hmm, how so, doll?"

"I hate when you're not touching me."

"Then I guess I'll have to do a better job of always being by you."

"You do know that is completely unrealistic, right?" I giggled, as he rolled us onto the couch, his body covering me.

"I already told you I'm going to lock you in my room and keep you naked. I don't think me touching you all the time is out of line." He leaned down, his lips brushing mine.

"You do realize we are on my sister's couch and she is fifteen feet away?"

"Does that mean you don't like this?" He nipped my earlobe and chills ran through me. "Or this?" He trailed kisses down my neck, and I arched my back, pressing into him, begging for more. "Then I guess I better stop." He pulled away from me, but I grabbed his shoulders and pulled him back.

"Just one more kiss," I whispered.

"There's always time for one more kiss," he whispered.

"OK, I've stayed out for as long as I can," Paige said, walking back into the room, her hand covering her eyes. "Please put all clothes on and get off my sister."

Gambler grunted and pulled away from me. He sat on the end of the couch and ran his fingers through his hair. "Sorry, Paige," he mumbled.

I sat up, a bit dazed, "Um, did you order the pizza?" I pulled my shirt down that I hadn't even realized Gambler had pulled up and swung my feet off the couch and sat up.

"Yeah, it should be here in half an hour. I figure if we keep working, we'll be done in no time and you shouldn't have to come back tomorrow."

By the time the pizza arrived, Paige had all her cows unpacked, Gambler was working on putting all the boxes in the rooms they belonged, and I was aimlessly unpacking the kitchen, still needing the man who had almost taken me on my sister's couch.

Gambler was wearing me down, making me rethink everything I thought I knew about him. Gambler was turning into the man I always wanted. I just hoped it stayed that way.

''*'*'*'*'*'*'*'*'*'*'*'*'*'*'*

Chapter 23

GAMBLER

"Leo just pulled up. Get your ass out here," King barked into the phone.

"I'll be right there." I hung the phone up and tossed it on the bedside table. I looked down at Gwen, who was sprawled out on top of me, quietly snoring.

She had spent all day at her sister's yesterday, leaving Marley to take care of the shop. Turtle had stayed with Gwen while I helped King and Demon get everything ready for Leo's sister Fayth and nephew coming today.

The past couple days had been busy and it seemed the only time we spent together was when we were sleeping. It was only seven thirty, and I already needed to leave her.

I slipped out from under her, careful not to wake her up, and laid her head on my pillow. She moaned in her sleep but grabbed the pillow and wrapped her arms around it. I didn't know what I did to get her in my bed, but I was going to do everything I could to keep her there.

After I had my clothes and boots on, I slipped back over to the bed and pressed a kiss to the side of her head and brushed her hair from her face. She looked like an angel when she slept, peaceful and carefree. I kissed her one last time, half hoping she would wake up, but didn't.

"It's about fucking time you haul your ass out of that room," Hammer called when I walked into the main room.

"Fuck off. You wouldn't want to leave your room either if you had what I do." I grabbed an empty cup and filled it with steaming coffee.

"Ha! You were the only one who had a chance with her. Lucky fucker," Hammer mumbled walking over to the bar. He grabbed a plate and piled it high with waffles, eggs, and bacon.

"Who the hell cooked?" My stomach growled as I saw Slider, Demon, and Gravel shoveling food into their mouths.

"Meg. She woke up, made breakfast and now she's back in bed," King explained walking into the kitchen with his empty plate.

"And I can tell you right now she is not a morning person. As soon as she walked out of her room this morning she threatened to stab me if I talked to her. Freaking crazy," Slider said as he picked up his coffee cup and walked over to the coffee pot.

"You might not want to talk smack about the chick who feeds you ninety percent of the time," Gravel laughed.

"Eh, not making fun, just giving out a warning." Slider shrugged his shoulders and took a sip of his coffee.

I walked over to the food and mounded my plate full, sat down at the table and tucked in to eat. "I thought Leo was here?" I asked, my mouth full, looking around.

"He should be here in half an hour. I remember how I was when Meg and I hooked up. I figured you would need the extra time to say goodbye."

"She was still sleeping. She's been working hard and then helping her sister getting settled in, I think she's been running on empty."

"You didn't tell her you were leaving?" King asked.

I shook my head no and forked in a load of eggs into my mouth. "She knew what I had going on today. She said she was just going to run to the salon with Marley to take care of a couple of appointments, and then she was just going to head back here and relax. I'm good."

King just shook his head and grinned. "If that's what you think, brother."

I don't know what the big deal was. I had let Marley know where I would be today, she seemed fine with it. I glanced at the clock seeing it was a quarter to eight. It probably wouldn't hurt to wake Gwen quick to say I was headed out.

"Yo! Leo is here," Turtle said, sticking his head into the door. Shit, there went telling Gwen I was leaving.

"Let's go. First stop is a couple of offices we found for him. Leo setting up an office in town could be a good thing." King set his cup down and headed out the door.

We all followed, Hammer piling up all our dishes and carrying them to the sink.

I glanced down the hall, thinking I could quick sneak down to our room, but if she woke up, I knew it wasn't going to be a quick kiss and then be gone. She was going to want me to stay, and I wouldn't want to leave.

I felt my pocket, making sure I had my phone and planned on calling her in a little bit when I knew she would be awake. That would have to do.

''*'*'*'*'*'*'*'*'*'*

Gwen

I woke up and I knew he wasn't in bed. I cracked one eye open and rolled over to look at the bathroom and saw the door open, Gambler not in there. I glanced at the clock and saw it was nine o'clock. Shit! I needed to be at the salon in fifteen minutes. I whipped the covers back and jumped out of bed.

After a quick brush of my hair and teeth, I swiped on some eyeshadow and I was rummaging through my bag trying to find something to wear.

"Hey, you ready to go?" Marley stuck her head into my room, a smile plastered on her face. Someone apparently didn't oversleep like I did.

"Yeah, I just need to throw some clothes on," I mumbled. I grabbed a vintage Betty Boop long sleeve tee and a pair of jeans and dashed back into the bathroom.

"The guys left pretty early this morning," Marley called through the door.

Well, at least, Marley knew what time the men left. I didn't even remember Gambler leaving the bed. Who knows if he even said goodbye. Yesterday at Paige's had worn me out. Although we finally had all her stuff put away, so it was definitely worth it. She was here to stay, and I couldn't be happier. "What time did they leave?" I pulled my shirt over my head and fluffed my hair. I needed a shower but didn't have time. I grabbed a stray bandana from the bottom of my bag and tied it up in my hair. "This is as good as it's going to get today," I said to the mirror and headed back to my suitcase to find shoes.

"Um, I think it was over an hour ago."

I opened my shoe suitcase and saw it was empty. What the hell? I glanced at the floor and saw ninety percent of my shoes were scattered around. Oh shit. When the hell did I get so messy? Normally I was so neat and orderly it drove people crazy. If I didn't know any better, it looked like Paige was staying here.

I spied my black Mary Jane's sticking out from under the bed, grabbed them and slid them on my feet. After I had got done at the salon, I was going to have to clean up. "OK, I'm ready. I just need a cup of coffee for the road and then we can hit it. Are we taking Troy's truck?" I asked as we walked down the hall.

"Yeah, he hates my car. Plus, I love his truck. It's a win, win," she laughed.

I grabbed a travel cup, filled it to the brim and snapped the lid on.

We headed out to the truck that Troy had idled at the door and climbed in. I rubbed my arms as I waited for Marley to get in and figured I should have grabbed a coat. We were having an unreasonably warm winter for Wisconsin, but it was still a bit chilly in the morning. I glanced at the clock on the dash and knew I didn't have time to run back in. Oh well, it looked like I would just have to turn the heat up a bit.

"How long is this going to take?" Troy asked as we headed out of the driveway.

"Probably two hours. I think we have six girls we need to do, although they all want pretty basic updos." I flipped the visor down and checked my face. I should have taken more time with my makeup. I always liked to go to work dressed up because my appearance represented what I was capable of, but I just didn't have the time this morning. "You don't like spending time with Marley when she's at work?"

"It's not that I don't like spending time with Marley, it's just that I never thought I would spend so much fucking time inside a salon. I come home smelling like hair dye and shampoo."

Marley reached over and patted his cheek. "Oh, my poor Troy. Does all this girl time bother you? Should I bring a football, baseball and some Penthouses the next time?"

"Yeah, just what I want to do, hold my balls, read porn and watch you cut hair. My life is complete." Troy rolled his eyes and grabbed Marley's hand. "It's a damn good thing I love you." He pressed a kiss to the back of her palm and held her hand in his lap. Marley leaned over and pressed a kiss to his cheek.

"I love you, too," she mumbled.

I looked out the window and rested my head against the glass. Son of a bitch, I missed Gambler. It had only been a couple of hours since he left to go take care of club business, and I felt like a clingy bitch because I was upset he didn't tell me he was leaving. Shit.

We pulled up in front of the shop as I scolded myself for being so dependent. I vowed to myself when Matt and I broke up that I would never rely on a man so much again. Now here I was moping around, pining after a guy again.

"Oh crap, they're early."

I glanced at the front of the shop and saw a group of woman crowded around the door, looking through the glass, none of them looking happy. I pushed my sunglasses up my nose and realized this was not going to be a good morning.

I was a sad sack pining over Gambler and now I had a feeling I was about to deal with Bridezilla. This day could be over any time now.

''*'*'*'*'*'*'*'*'*'*'*'*

Chapter 24

GAMBLER

"Man, this is the fourth fucking office building we've looked at. You think he's ever going to pick one?" Hammer sat next to me in one of the shop's trucks, eating a banana. Don't ask me where the hell he got a banana from.

"Well, seeing as this is the last available building in Rockton, this one is going to be it or nothing."

"We've been at this shit for four hours and we still have to help move his sister in. We're not gonna be done till fucking dinner time and I'm fucking starving." Hammer chomped down on his banana, chewing with his mouth open. I swear he had ten brain cells and five of them were slowly dimming.

"First off, chew with your fucking mouth shut." I reached over and smacked him in the back of the head. "Secondly, this shit better not take that long. I forgot to plug my phone in last night and the motherfucker died before we even made it to the first office."

"You can use mine if you want." Hammer patted his left pocket and his eyes grew big. He patted his right pocket. "Shit, I must have left it back at the clubhouse."

I shook my head and ran my fingers through my hair. Son of a bitch. I didn't know if Gwen was going to be pissed or understand why I hadn't called her all day. "No worries, brother. I just wanted to check in with Gwen."

"You two finally together, huh?" Hammer wiggled his eyebrows at me as he took an enormous bite.

"Yeah, for the most part."

"What the hell does that mean? She warms your bed every night."

"Yeah, she does, but…" I ran my fingers through my hair again and sighed.

"But what? What else is there?"

"A whole lot more, brother, but I don't know if Gwen wants to give me more."

Hammer's jaw dropped open and he gaped at me. "Holy shit, not you too. You're gonna be like King and Rigid, aren't you?"

"King and Rigid got a good thing, brother. Nothing wrong with wanting what they have, especially if it's with someone like Gwen." I pictured Gwen lying in bed this morning when I left, and I knew that was what I wanted to wake up to every morning.

"If you say so. I think I'm going to stick with my bike and freedom." Hammer folded up the banana peel and tossed it out the window. "Having one woman holds ya down, and that's not something I want."

"To each their own, brother." I turned my head, looked out the window and saw King, Demon, and Leo finally walk out of the office building. Besides Hammer and I keeping an eye on things, Leo also had his own men riding along today. Leo said he hadn't heard anything from the Assassins since

187

Troy had been kidnapped, but he was very cautious that they were now going to go after Leo.

Going after Leo and the Banachi's would be a huge mistake, but as we had seen in the past, the assassins were not a smart bunch. Things had been quiet since they had tried to kill Gwen and I. We still didn't know if they were going after anyone in the Knights now, or if they again mistook the wrong people for Rigid and Cyn.

King walked over to our truck and I rolled the window down. "He's going with this one. It's not exactly what he wanted, but he said he can make the improvements needed."

"Nice. So, now what? Is the sister in town yet?" I asked, grabbing my pack of smokes and pulled one out.

"Yeah, he said she was about three hours behind in the U-Haul. She's been at the house for almost an hour now. We head over there, help get her all set up and then we can head back to the clubhouse."

"Sweet. You good with riding with Gravel?"

"Yeah, we're good. He's a grumpy fucking bear right now, but I can handle it."

"What the hell is up his ass? He hasn't seemed too happy these past couple of weeks." Gravel had walked into the clubhouse this morning acting like someone had pissed in his cheerios.

"Not sure, brother. I'll try to talk to him and see if he'll tell me anything. I know we're all getting sick of looking over our shoulders so maybe that's just got him wound tight right now."

"Could be." I glanced over King's shoulder and saw Leo sitting in his car, waiting. "We better head out." I nodded at Leo and King turned around.

King patted the top of the truck and walked over to Gravel. "What do you think has got Gravel so ticked?" Hammer asked as I started the truck.

"Don't know, brother. Could be a bunch of shit, or it could be Gravel just being Gravel."

"Yeah, you're probably right." Hammer reached down into the side of the door and pulled out another banana.

"Dude, where the hell are you getting these bananas from?" I asked, shocked as he pulled out two more.

"I knew it was going to be a long day, so I grabbed the bunch of bananas that was sitting on the counter before we left. Pretty smart, huh?' He peeled another banana and ate half of it in one bite.

Yeah, Hammer wasn't going to think he was very smart when he got back to the clubhouse and Meg rips him a new asshole for eating all the bananas she was going to use to make banana cream bars. "Yeah, you sure are a smart one," I laughed, shifting into drive and followed behind Leo and his goons.

We headed in the direction of Fayth's house while Hammer rambled on about all the benefits of eating bananas.

"Dude, these suckers are loaded with potassium. One of these and…"

I tuned out Hammer, knowing he was just rambling and not looking for a response. I glanced at the clock on the dash and groaned. The more time that went by, the more I doubted Gwen would be OK with me not calling her. I was sure she had probably called me, but there was no way for me to know until I got my phone charged.

Let's hope when I got back to the clubhouse Gwen wasn't ready to rip me a new asshole like Meg was going to do to Hammer.

''*'*'*'*'*'*'*'*'*'*

Gwen

"Who the hell eats a whole bunch of bananas? Like, I'm talking a big bunch of bananas. At least 9!" Meg flailed her arms around as she yelled and searched the kitchen for the mysterious missing bananas.

"I feel like this is a case for Scooby Doo and the gang," Cyn laughed, plopping down on a stool by the bar.

"This is not a time to make jokes," Meg called from the kitchen.

I was standing in the doorway to the kitchen, exhausted from a long day of dealing with Bridezilla, but I was thoroughly entertained at the moment. "I haven't seen Scooby Doo in ages. Is it still on TV?" I asked.

"Oh yeah. It's definitely still on. I make Rigid watch it with me sometimes. He always bitched because I make him watch the new episodes and he says they have nothing on the old ones." Cyn grabbed her glass of water and took a drink.

Marley stood on the other side of the bar from Cyn, her head propped in her hand as she leaned against the bar. "I always had a thing for Shaggy."

Cyn spit her water out and slammed her glass down. Meg leaned out the doorway to the kitchen and we all stared at Marley. "What the hell did you say?" Cyn asked, wiping water off her chin.

Marley wiped her hand off that was covered with water with a bar towel and handed it to Cyn. "Um, I had a thing for Shaggy?"

"You do realize Shaggy is a cartoon, right?" Meg asked.

"Of course," she propped her hands on her hips and stared us down. "Come on. You mean to tell me there's not a cartoon character that ya'll don't think is hot?"

Cyn, Meg and I looked at each other and shrugged our shoulders. "Well, I guess if you put it that way." Meg tapped her finger on her chin and hummed. "I suppose I'd have to go with Batman. He's all tall, dark, and handsome."

"Eh, I'm going with the Hulk," Cyn said as she propped her feet up on the stool in front of her.

"Dude, you just looked at me like I was insane for saying Shaggy, but you just named a huge, nine foot, lime green giant who gets pissed off then transforms into said monster." Marley shook her head and grabbed the towel, tossing it into the sink.

Cyn held her hands up and shrugged. "I can't help what I like."

"That would explain why she's into Rigid. I swear we should have painted him green for Halloween and made him pass out candy as the Hulk," I said, walking into the kitchen.

"I am so making him do that after I pop this baby out," Cyn giggled, rubbing her belly.

I grabbed a bag of chips and the huge bowl of guacamole Meg had made earlier and headed to the bar. "Question," I said, ripping open the bag of chips. "Who the hell dyes his hair?"

"I do now. Before me, he said he did it himself, although I have a sneaky suspicion he either had one of the club girls do it or Demon."

"Demon? Why the hell would you say that?" Meg asked, walking behind the bar, grabbing bottles and setting them on the top.

"Because Demon mentioned a couple of weeks ago to Rigid that it looked like he was due to have his hair dyed. Now, you tell me why the hell he would say that?"

"I am so picturing Rigid sitting in the bathroom, on the toilet, a towel draped over his shoulders and Demon rubbing blue shit in his hair," Meg laughed.

Marley and Cyn burst out laughing, and I couldn't help but laugh too. "Oh my god," I groaned.

"Ugh, not the picture I wanted. I'd like to believe Rigid and Demon are more manly than that." Marley dipped her chip in the guacamole and moaned. "This is the best shit, ever."

"Yeah, well, you should try my banana cream bars. Wait, you can't because someone ate all the fucking bananas!" Meg yelled, her eyes traveling over all of us.

"Ugh, and now we're back to the bananas," Cyn laughed, shaking her head.

"I can tell you right now there is no way I could eat nine bananas, so turn your eyes elsewhere," I said, wagging my fingers at her.

"Well, I can tell you one thing, I am going to find out who ate my bananas, and when I do they will pay."

Cyn laughed and loaded her chip with a mound of guacamole. "Sure you will. More like just make them run to the store and buy you more."

"Hey, you never said who you thought was hot as a cartoon," Marley said, pointing her finger at me. Meg and Cyn both nodded their heads as they chewed.

"Oh, that's easy. Johnny Bravo all the way." Couldn't tell I'd ever thought about this before.

"Isn't that the guy with the oddly shaped body and way blonde hair?" Meg asked.

"Yeah."

"I have no idea who the hell that is," Marley said.

"You're kidding me. Someone grab their phone and educate Marley here. Shaggy has nothing on Johnny Bravo." Cyn pulled her phone out of her pocket and asked Google who Johnny Bravo is.

"Why the hell are you googling Johnny Bravo?" Troy asked, walking into the common room.

"Because Gwen had the hots for him," Meg said, walking past Troy and into the kitchen.

"He's a cartoon," Troy said, confused.

"Well, in that case, you *really* don't want to know who Marley had a thing for," Cyn said, rolling her eyes.

"Who the hell is it? I bet it's Batman, isn't it?" Troy crossed his arms over his chest and stared down Marley.

"Dude! That was mine!" Meg yelled from the kitchen.

"I should have known," Troy mumbled.

"You're never going to guess it," Cyn mumbled.

"OK!" Marley yelled. "It's Shaggy, alright? I never thought it was weird until I told these three."

Troy threw his head back and laughed. "I always had a thing for Velma."

Cyn's jaw dropped. "You're kidding me. You two are like a match made in heaven."

Troy walked around the bar and wrapped his arms around Marley. "It's only a little weird you had the hots for Shaggy," Troy mumbled.

"Oh! Here, I've got Johnny Bravo!" Cyn held her phone up and shoved it in Marley's face.

Marley grabbed the phone and laughed. "At least, Shaggy looks human, this guy has a triangle for a body and like no facial features."

I grabbed the phone out of her hands and scoffed. "Come on, he thought all the ladies wanted him and he had confidence for days." Although I did have to admit, I remembered him a bit differently.

"Lo just texted me. He said they'll be here in ten minutes." Meg walked out of the kitchen, her nose buried in her phone.

I pulled my phone out, wondering if I had missed a call from Gambler but there was nothing. I had called him more than five times today, but it went to voicemail each time. Each time I called him, I got a little bit more pissed off.

"Nothing yet?" Marley asked.

I shook my head no and shoved my phone back in my pocket. "It's nothing. He told me he was going to be busy today."

"Yeah, well, the prick could have at least called once." We all looked at Cyn, shocked. "Hey," she said, holding her hands up. "I just call it like I seem 'em."

"Damn, Cyn is one friend you want on your side," Marley laughed.

"Yeah, she definitely is a ride or die bitch." Meg put her arm around Cyn's shoulders and laughed.

"You putting the moves on my woman?" We all turned around to see Rigid standing in the doorway, smirking.

"Well, if you wouldn't leave her alone so much I wouldn't have to."

Rigid looked at his wrist, "I've only been gone seven hours."

"Since when did you get a watch?" Cyn asked.

Rigid laughed and held up his arm that didn't have a watch on it. "You got me."

"King just called and said ten minutes. What the hell are you doing here?" Meg asked.

"I left a couple of minutes before they did. I hitched a ride with Gambler and Hammer. Never again will I do that. The three of us crammed into that truck was not a good idea. Plus, I kept stepping on banana peels." Rigid walked over to Cyn and put his hands on her belly. "How's my little biker?" he mumbled.

"I knew it! Your boyfriend ate all of my bananas!" Meg turned around glaring and pointing at me.

"Hey! Gambler is his own man."

"I'm gonna beat the bananas out of him," Meg threatened.

"Who, Hammer?" I whirled around at Gambler's voice and smiled. I was still annoyed he hadn't called me all day, but dammit did he look good. He still hadn't shaved and he was wearing his signature jeans, tee, and boots. Plus, a leather coat since the weather had turned cold. Although, if you looked at any of the guys in the club, that seemed to be standard attire. Except they all appeared to have their own spin on it.

"What the hell does Hammer have to do with you eating all my bananas?"

"The fact that I had to sit in that god damn truck all day watching him mow down on them."   "Oh, shit." Meg turned her head to me. "I take back what I said."

"What the hell did Meg say now?" King asked, walking in from the shop. He closed the door behind him and took his coat off. Leather jackets seemed to be another thing the guys all added to their uniforms in the winter time.

"Someone ate all my bananas and I'm pretty sure it was Hammer."

"I wouldn't doubt it. The fucker is a god damn garbage disposal."

I tuned everyone out when Gambler started walking over to me. Remember you're mad at him, Gwen, I reminded myself. But the closer he got, the more my anger disappeared and all I wanted was to be in his arms.

"Nice of you to call."

"I tried, doll." He pulled his phone out of his pocket and handed it to me. "I forgot to plug it in last night. It died an hour after I left and I was stuck with Hammer all day. Motherfucker left his here."

"You couldn't borrow someone else's?" I crossed my arms over my chest and cocked my hip out.

"Well, if you're going to play that way, doll, if you were really concerned you couldn't have had Meg call King to talk to me?" Gambler crossed his arms, mimicking me.

My blood boiled, pissed the hell of by the fact he thinks I should have tried harder to talk to him. "So you mess up, and I have to go out of my way to talk to you? I was busy at work today and didn't have time to try to play leap frog on the damn phone."

Gambler took a step towards me, closing the distance between us. His eyes darkened and he grabbed my arm, "You might want to be careful what you say next, doll. I've been on edge all day not able to talk to you and now when I can, all I get is sass."

I tugged my arm, trying to get away, but he tightened his grip and pulled my body flush against him. He plastered his hand to my ass and held me close. I looked up, his face tilted down at me. "Don't be a dick, Gambler," I spat out. He was cranky he couldn't talk to me, well, so was I.

"You got one more try, doll," he warned.

"Dick!" I shouted in his face.

Gambler growled low, and I knew I might have made a mistake. "Bad move," he whispered. He pushed me away, surprising me so I stumbled over my feet, and he put his shoulder in my stomach and lifted me up. "What the hell are you doing? I don't want to go anywhere with you!" I pounded on his back but he didn't stop.

"I warned you twice. I'm not taking your sass about this." He swatted me on the ass and headed down the hallway. "Anyone knocks on our door, all they're going to meet is my fist," Gambler growled as we walked past everyone by the bar. I really couldn't see them except for their feet, though.

"Whoa, Hulk smash," Cyn yelled.

"What the hell does that mean?" I heard Rigid ask.

"Your girl has got a thing for the Hulk." I heard Meg say as we turned the corner down the hall. I really wish I could have heard what Rigid's reaction was.

"Gambler, put me down. I can God damn walk."

"You won't be able to when I get done with you." He reached into his pocket and pulled his keys out. I swatted at his hand and he dropped them. He went still and this was the second time in five minutes I regretted my actions. "You're really trying my patience today, Gwen."

"Sorry," I gulped.

"I think you need to be taught a lesson," He growled. He set me down on my feet and pressed me against the wall. He caged me in with his arms and body making it so there was no escape. I looked up and down the hallway, hoping one of the girls had followed us, but they hadn't.

"No one is coming to save you, doll." My eyes snapped to his and a shiver ran through my body. I swallowed hard, a little terrified, but a whole lot turned on.

"I'm not sure if I want to be saved," I whispered.

Gambler growled low and slammed his lips down on mine. His fingers delved into my hair, pulling my bandana off, tossing it on the floor. He tilted my head back, his lips devouring me. I held on to his arms and moaned as his tongue snaked into my mouth. "Wrap your legs around me," he mumbled against my lips. He grabbed my ass and I swung my legs around his waist as he pressed me against the wall. "Why can't I get enough of you?"

I pressed my lips to his, not wanting to answer. I knew the reason why I couldn't get enough of him, I was falling in love with him. Did Gambler feel the same way? I didn't have a clue. "Maybe we should take this in your room."

"Not yet," he mumbled, trailing kisses down my neck. He grabbed the hem of my shirt and yanked it over my head.

"Whoa, whoa," I protested. I crossed my arms over my chest and looked down the hallway. "Gambler, what if someone comes down the hall?'

"No one is coming down here. I told them to leave us the fuck alone."

I pushed on his shoulder and he lifted his head. "No, you told him not to knock on our door. Last I checked," I looked up and down the hall, "we're not in your room."

"Gwen."

"What?'

"Shut up." His lips claimed mine again and all thought except for Gambler left me. I wrapped my arms around his neck and held on. I arched my hips, squeezing my legs tighter around him. His hands kneaded my breasts through my bra, and I moaned as he raised my bra and his head lowered. His mouth sought out my nipple and I ran my fingers through his hair.

"Yes," I moaned as he rocked his hips against me. "I need you, Gambler."

"I'm gonna set you down and you have ten seconds to get your pants off, OK?"

I nodded my head yes, unable to talk. I was about to have sex in a hallway that anyone could walk down, and all I could think about was how fast I could get my pants off.

My feet touched the floor, and I ripped open the fly of my jeans, slid down the zipper and tore them down my legs. Thankfully I had slipped on a pair of flats when I got home so they just fell off when I pushed my jeans down.

Gambler had his pants pulled down to his knees, and he was stroking his dick as he watched me. "You're mine," he growled as he stroked one last time. He prowled to me, his hands grabbing my ass and he hoisted me up. "Ride me."

I didn't have to be told twice. I reached down, stroking his rock, hard dick. He leaned back, and I guided his cock in and slowly sunk down on him. I threw my head back and moaned as he reached places that drove me insane. Gambler kissed my neck as he kneaded my ass. "Ah, I don't know how you do it, Gambler."

"Do what, doll?" He sucked on my neck, driving me, even more, crazy.

"All I can see is you. You make the world disappear." I buried my fingers in his hair, lifting his head to mine. "What have you done to me?"

"I'm making you fall in love with me. I'm not letting you go. Stop questioning it, and just let go." He kissed me long and deep, giving me everything I needed in just that one kiss. Gambler had just said he wasn't going to let me go, and I wasn't freaking out, trying to figure out how to push him away. "You ready to ride me?"

"God yes," I moaned. I steadied myself by putting my hands on his shoulders and used my legs wrapped around him as leverage and pulled myself up. Gambler gritted his teeth and put his hands under my ass and helped to lift me up.

"Fuck, you're like a fucking vise like this," he groaned as I slid back down. "Fuck," he said, closing his eyes.

I lifted up again and slid back down, over and over. My climax built with each movement as I slammed down on his dick, faster and faster. "I need to cum," I breathed out, "please."

"Not yet, doll, not yet," Gambler chanted as he took over, thrusting up as I slammed down. "I want you to cum all over my dick while I cum inside you. Together," he growled. His lips claimed mine, taking everything I had to give.

"Who do you belong to?" he asked against my lips. "Tell me."

"You," I whispered.

"Louder. I need to hear it."

"You, I belong to you," I moaned on the brink of ecstasy.

"I can't let you go, I need you." I fell over the edge at his words. Words I needed to hear. My orgasm slammed into me, taking my breath away. Gambler threw his head back groaning as he fell over the edge with me. He slowing thrusted, the walls of my pussy pulsing and contracting as I milked every drop of cum from him.

He stumbled forward, my back hitting the wall. "Holy fuck," he gasped, catching his breath.

I leaned forward, wrapping my arms around him and held on. I loved Gambler, and I was going to hold on like I could lose him at any second.

''*'*'*'*'*'*'*'*'*

Chapter 25

GAMBLER

"We should really get in your room," Gwen mumbled into my chest.

"I'm not sure my legs will make it." I had my knees locked and was sure as soon as I tried to walk, I was going to fall over. Gwen had taken everything I had to give, and I was drained to the point of exhaustion.

"Set me down, you grab the key and we can haul ass into the room."

I shook my head no and buried my face in her hair. "Five more-."

"Meg, stay the hell away from their room!" We heard called. My head snapped back and I looked at Gwen whose eyes were bugged out.

"Fuck," she whispered, hitting me in the shoulder. "Let me the hell down!" She dropped her legs from my waist, and I unlocked my knees and scrambled to find the key. Apparently while we were going at it, I must have kicked it. My eyes darted all over, hoping to glance the white key fob and saw it ten feet down the hall. I lunged for it, my fucking pants still around my knees.

"Quick!" Gwen whispered, panicking to grab her shirt and bra.

"Someone needs to check on her! Gambler was a dick to her." Meg whined, her voice getting closer. I sprinted to the door, Gwen at my back as I fumbled with the key and finally got it in the lock and twisted the handle open. Gwen pushed me in and we landed in a heap on the floor. Gwen kicked her leg, connecting with the door and it swung shut.

"That was close," Gwen laughed, laying down next to me.

"We still had about ten seconds." I reached over and pulled Gwen to my side. She rested her head on my shoulder and looked up at me.

"I suppose you think ten seconds is a long time."

"It doesn't even sound like King let her down here." We both listened, our breathing the only thing we heard. "He must have headed her off at the turn in the hall."

"Thank God," Gwen murmured.

"I'm sorry I didn't call you today, doll." I looked into her beautiful face and a grin spread across her lips.

"You don't sound like the guy outside my door five minutes ago who demanded I shut up and fucked me breathless."

"You do crazy things to me, doll. Your attitude drives me insane. All I want to do is fuck it out of you when you start mouthing off." I brushed her hair out of her face and slid my thumb over her soft lips. "I meant what I said out there. I'm not letting you go, even if you want to leave. I'll just have to find ways to convince you to love me."

"I think you're crazy, but I don't think I'll need much convincing to stick around," I smirked, biting his thumb.

"Oh yeah?" I laughed. I reached over, tickling her side and she squealed, pushing my hand away.

"No, you don't fight fair!" she laughed, fighting me.

"Gwen!" Shit, I guess King didn't hold Meg off.

"Stop it," she hissed at me. "Meg is going to think you're hurting me."

"Yeah, because people always laugh when they are getting hurt," I laughed, both hands attacking her now. I rolled her over, pinning her to the floor and straddled her hips. "I'm not letting you up until you get rid of Meg."

"You're crazy," she gasped as I doubled my efforts. "I'm fine, Meg. Gambler's just yelling at me."

"What?" Meg called.

"Why you little liar." I grabbed her arms and pinned them over her head. "You better tell her the truth before I turn you over my knee and give you the spanking you deserve."

"Never," she laughed, wiggling underneath me. "Gambler says he's going to spank me, Meg!"

I held her wrists with one hand and put my other hand over her mouth. "Did you just lick me?" I asked, pulling my hand away.

"Fair warning. You put your hand on my mouth, you will get licked." She stuck her tongue out at me and bucked her hips trying to get out from under me.

"King, get over here!" Meg called.

"Oh shit, you're in trouble now, she's getting King," Gwen taunted.

"Oh yeah, watch this."

"Gambler," King said.

"Yo!"

"You good?"

"Never better. Just working the attitude out of Gwen." Gwen squeaked, outraged. "We'll be out for dinner in a couple of minutes."

"Get, now," I heard King mumble. I heard Meg stomp down the hallway, their voices fading.

"You do know my attitude, as you put it, is not going anywhere, right?"

I let go of Gwen's wrists and cupped my hands around her face. "I hope not, it's one of my favorite things about you." I leaned down and gently pressed a kiss to her lips.

"What else do you like about me?"

"You fishing for compliments, doll?"

"No, it's just nice to hear sometimes what you like about me."

"All right," I said, leaning back. "One, you have legs for days. I'm talking you could wrap 'em around me twice." Gwen laughed, her cheeks blushing. "Two, your fucking hair. I have no idea what the hell you do to it, but I seriously want to bury my face in it every time you're near."

"It's shampoo, Gambler," she laughed.

"Yeah, well, I think it's also you, too. You make everything better."

"I think you're just partial because I'm warming your bed right now."

"Wrong. You are more than warming my bed."

"Then what the hell am I doing?"

"Becoming part of my life."

"Don't you think it's a little too soon to be talking like that? We've known each other what, a month, five weeks?"

"Well, you are meeting my mom tomorrow, so I would have to say that means something." I had made plans to see her last week, but Gwen had to work late and we couldn't make it.

"Ugh, I feel like I'm going to puke every time you mention meeting your mom. Can't we do that like next year?"

"You do realize that this is the middle of November and next year isn't that far off, right?"

"Well, even if we only wait that long I'll be fine."

"Gwen," I growled, "we're having dinner with my mom tomorrow. I want you to be there."

"You need a haircut," she said, sitting up. She reached up and brushed her fingertips against the ends of my hair.

"Stop trying to distract me." I turned my head and kissed her palm. "I don't want to wait, Gwen. You never know what is going to happen in life. If anything taught me that, it was losing Evie. She was here one day and then she was gone the next. I'm not letting that happen to me again."

"You can't guarantee I'll be here, Gambler."

"That's not what I mean. I just know that the time I do have, I want to make the most of it. I want to know that if I were to die tomorrow, I wouldn't have any regrets."

"You think I could be a regret you have? You could regret giving me so much time down the road."

"Gwen, stop trying to talk me out of wanting to spend time with you."

She rolled her eyes and crossed her arms over her chest. "I'm not doing that; I just don't see why we have to rush into things."

"And I don't see why we just can't be together already. I want you and you want me. What the hell is holding you back? I'm all in, Gwen. It's time for you to place your bet. Are you here, doing this with me, or are you going to disappear once we get all the Assassin shit sorted out?"

She pushed my chest, knocking me to the side and scrambled off the floor. She grabbed her bra and slid her arms into it. "I need some air, Gambler. We went from just having fun to have a discussion about the rest of my life. I can't decide this so easily."

"That's the thing, Gwen, this should be an easy answer. I don't doubt it for a second that I want to be with you."

"Well good for you, Gambler. I'm sorry that I'm not as decisive as you are." She grabbed her jeans and hopped from one foot to the other as she pulled them on.

"You're blowing this way out of proportion, Gwen. You're acting like I've announced we're getting married."

Gwen just shook her head and shoved her feet into her shoes. "I can't do this right now."

I jumped up from the floor and grabbed her. "Then when the hell are you going to be able to do it, Gwen? Why can't you just say you want to be with me?"

"Because I've already done that once in my life and it was a huge mistake. I don't think I can do it again."

"You know what is really crazy about this whole thing?" She shook her head no and pulled out of my arms. "I have no idea what you are talking about. How am I supposed to be different from what you had in the past if I don't know what happened? I'm pitted against something I can't fight because I have no idea what it is."

"I need to go, Gambler. I need to get out of here." She ran her fingers through her hair and looked around like a caged animal.

I had no idea what was going through her head right now. We were fine and then we weren't. "You can't leave by yourself right now, Gwen."

"Then someone can come with me."

"Just let me get my shirt on and-"

"No! Someone that isn't you. I'm just going to go to the salon."

"What the hell are you going to do at the salon right now? It's closed."

Gwen shook her head and stepped to the door. "I own the fucking salon, Gambler, I can go there whenever I want, closed or not. I'll meet you out at the bar." She twisted the door handle, tossed it open and took off down the hall.

I looked around the room trying to figure what the hell just happened. I didn't even know what to do. I was fighting something I didn't even do.

I grabbed my boots, laced them up and grabbed my keys. If Gwen didn't want to be with me right now, she was, at least, going to have one of the brothers with her. I headed down the hall and my eyes searched for Gwen, but I didn't see her.

"Where the hell did Gwen go?" I asked King.

"She said she was going to wait in the car for you."

"Son of a bitch," I ran to the door just in time to see her taillights pull out of the driveway. "Fuck!"

"What the hell is going on?" King walked over, Meg behind him.

"I don't have a fucking clue."

"Well, where the hell is she going? She's by herself." Meg pushed past King and I and looked down the street.

"Shit, I should go after her, but she said she doesn't want to be with me right now." Son of a bitch. I knew she was mad at me right now, but why the hell did she have to leave?

"Demon," King called. Demon walked out from behind the bar and over to King. "I'm gonna need you to follow Gwen."

"Where the hell did she go?" he asked, pulling his keys out of his pocket.

"She said she wanted to go to the salon. I would head there." I pulled my phone out, wanting to send her a message but the fucking thing was dead. "God dammit!" I chucked my phone across the parking lot and it smashed against the dumpster by the ditch. This all started because of my fucking phone. Now I couldn't even call her because the damn thing was still dead.

"I'll keep an eye on her," Demon mumbled. He walked over to one of the shop trucks and took off.

"So what the hell did you do to her?" Meg asked, her hands propped on her hips.

"I didn't do a damn thing other than telling her I want to fucking be with her."

"So she just took off? That doesn't make any sense!" Meg bitched.

"It makes sense to me," King said, walking over to Meg. "Head back in babe. I'm gonna talk to Gambler for a bit."

"I don't want to. All I want to do is kick Gambler in the nuts right now for hurting Gwen." Meg glared at me so now I not only had Gwen pissed off at me, now Meg was too.

"I didn't do anything to her, Meg. I fucking swear. All I wanted to do was take her to see my mom tomorrow and she freaked out, saying we were rushing things."

King grabbed Meg and whispered something in her ear. She stomped her foot and pointed her finger at King. "You better be right," she said. She stomped past me, glaring the whole time.

I pulled out a cigarette and stuck it in the corner of my mouth. I patted my pocket for my lighter and realized I left it in the truck. "Catch," King said, tossing one to me.

"What the hell do you have a lighter for?" I asked as I lit the end.

"It was sitting on the end of the bar. I figured it was Hammer's so I grabbed it to fuck with him," King smirked.

"Thanks," I muttered.

"So, that really all that happened with Gwen?"

"Yeah. I told her I didn't want to dick around anymore. I want to fucking be with her and she freaked. Told me she didn't know if she was ready for that. Something how she had been fucked over before."

"Meg did the same fucking thing."

"Oh yeah, that why you laid off of her for a bit?" We had all known that Meg and King had taken a break, but we never really knew why.

"She kept pinning all the shit her ex did on me. Even though I hadn't even done anything. Shit was whacked in her head. She needed to work through that shit before I could even think about being with her for good."

"I don't even know what the hell happened to her before me. She never mentioned anything about an ex. It's fucking bullshit."

"She'll come around, brother. You just need to give her some time."

"Fuck that. I'm not waiting weeks for her to come back to me. No offense, King, but two weeks is fourteen days too long." Wait two fucking weeks to talk to Gwen? I don't fucking think so.

"I'm not saying you need to wait that long, but don't go at her half-cocked, pissed off at the world. All that is going to do is push her away more."

"I'm not fucking pissed; I just want to know what the fuck is going on!"

"Yeah, you don't sound pissed at all," King laughed. "Look, go after her if you want, but you need to fucking listen to what she wants instead of telling her what you want." King patted me on the back and headed back into the clubhouse.

I looked up at the sky and had no idea what the fuck I was going to do. King was right in everything he said, but I couldn't wait. I had no idea what the hell it was that had Gwen running. The Gwen I had come to know would never run from something.

I needed to find out what the fuck was going on.

''*'*'*'*'*'*'*'*'*'*'*

Chapter 26

Gwen

I needed to order more bleach and rubber gloves. I chewed the end of the pen and glanced around the shop. I had only turned on the back lights over the supply area and the rest of the salon was dimly lit.

Demon had pulled up in front of the shop over two hours ago. He had knocked on the door, told me he would be out front if he needed me and that was where he had stayed.

I had done inventory on everything in the shop, and now I had nothing to distract me from thinking about Gambler. I had run, plain and simple. He had scared the shit out of me with talk of his mom. He had mentioned it before, but I had ended up working late so I was hoping it would be forgotten. Obviously not.

I plopped down in a chair and slowly spun myself around. Time to sort shit out in my head.

Question 1. Was I over Matt? (I had to start at the root of my problem.)

Answer. Hell Yes.

Question 2. Was I over what Matt did to me? i.e. Lie for *years*.

Answer. Undecided. Although I was over Matt, I think I really wasn't over the fact someone could lie to me for so long, and I was the idiot that couldn't tell. I think that was what I was most worried about happening again. If Gambler lied to me, I probably wouldn't be able to tell. Apparently when I love someone, I'm blinded to the point where I think they're perfect.

So, was I over what Matt had done to me? No.

Question 3. Gambler hadn't lied to me yet, so why was I punishing him for what Matt had done to me?

Answer. Because I was too fucking terrified it would happen again. Damn Matt. He really screwed me up.

Question 4. Did I want to be with Gambler? (This question was a dousey.)

Answer. Yes. Wait, did I really just admit to it that fast? I put my foot down and stopped spinning. I think I had just had a major breakthrough.

I wanted to be with Gambler. I really did. Now how the hell was I going to tell him that after I basically just ran away?

I looked out the window and saw another shop truck pull up. Fuck. Gambler got out and walked over to Demon. Looked like I wasn't going to have to wait very long to tell Gambler. Shit.

''*'*'*'*'*'*'*'*'*'*

GAMBLER

I lasted a whole two hours before I couldn't take it anymore.

"Dammit, you couldn't have waited another twenty minutes before you showed up?" Demon cursed as I walked up to his truck.

"Two hours was long enough. Who won the bet?" I knew those fuckers back at the clubhouse would find some way to bet on my misery.

"Fucking Speed won. Cyn, Meg, and Marley even got in on the action. The pot was fucking big, brother. It would have been nice to have that extra cushion in my wallet."

"What she been up to in there?" I asked, looking over my shoulder at the salon.

"Looked like she was counting shit for a while, and she just sat down a couple of minutes ago. And from the look on her face, I'd say she just saw you."

"Yeah, I think you might be right," I laughed. Gwen was sitting in one of the barber chairs, sprawled out on it, her foot pushing her back and forth. Her arms were crossed over her chest and she looked pissed. "Maybe I should drive around the block a couple of times. See if she'll cool off a bit more."

She got up from the chair, walked to the front door, unlocked it and sat back down. "I'm pretty sure she wants you to go in. Now, I can't tell if she wants to apologize or kill you," Demon laughed.

"Alright, you staying here or heading back?"

"I'll hang here for a bit. Maybe grab some Chinese from down the street."

"Sounds good, I might need you for backup if Gwen decides to kick my ass."

Demon laughed and started up the truck. "I think you'll be good, brother, just listen to her. I'm gonna grab some food, and I'll be back."

Demon headed down the street, and I turned back to the salon. Gwen was staring me down, waiting. I crossed the street and stood in front of the door. "Just listen," I mumbled to myself.

I pulled the door open and locked it behind me.

"Making it so I can't get out?"

"Um, no. Making it so *I* can't get out."

"Hmm," she hummed. I sat down in the chair next to her and spun around so I was facing her.

"Get some work done?"

"I did inventory. I haven't done it since summer, so it needed to be done."

I nodded my head and slowly spun around in my chair. "I was worried about you."

"You didn't need to, I had Demon watching me."

"I know. King sent him. He was worried about you being alone."

She put her foot on my chair when I was face to face with her, stopping me from spinning. "King sent him or you did?"

"King did, although if he hadn't, I would have."

"Why did you come then if you knew that Demon was making sure I was safe?"

"I came to collect on the two bets you lost." A grin spread across my lips as it dawned on her I could ask her to do anything I wanted. Twice.

"You don't play fair, Gambler."

"I never said I did, doll."

She crossed her arms over her chest and stared me down. Even pissed off Gwen was hot. "Spit it out, what do you want?"

"Well," I ran my fingers through my hair and grinned. "I could use a haircut, free of charge of course."

"That's what you want, a haircut?"

"For the first one, don't forget about the second bet you lost."

Gwen growled but didn't say anything. She got up from her chair and walked to the mirror that was in front of my chair. "I have to admit I didn't think you were going to say haircut."

"Well, I figured, we're in a salon, you're a hairdresser, what better place to do it?"

She grabbed a cape, shook it out and snapped it over my shoulders. "I guess I can't argue with that logic." She spun me around to face the mirror and ran her fingers through my hair. "How short do you want it?"

"Up to you, doll. I trust you." She hummed as she grabbed a comb, spray bottle and scissors from the counter and wet my hair. "Now, time for the second bet you lost."

"Really, while I'm cutting your hair?" She set the spray bottle down, and started cutting.

"Yeah, I think it's a perfect time."

"You know I could accidently chop off all your hair right now?"

"There's that attitude I love so much."

"Hmm, just spit out what you want."

"Tell me why you're scared. Tell me why you ran. Tell me who the hell I have to beat up for making you doubt falling in love with me."

Her scissors stopped mid cut and her eyes connected with mine. "Ugh, that's three questions."

"Tell me, Gwen. I want to know. I need to know."

She licked her lips and looked back at my hair. She started cutting my hair again, but didn't talk. It took her almost five minutes before she said anything. "His name was Matt."

"Tell me more, doll."

"I met him when I was a teenager. He moved next door to me when I was fifteen. I fell in love with him the second I saw him." I growled low in my throat, but didn't say anything.

"I was with him for six years."

"That's a mighty long time, doll."

"Yeah," she murmured. "Six years too long." She worked on my hair, cutting the sides, combing them over. "Everything was good for five years. Matt was the perfect boyfriend. He's the one who got me into riding. The first time I rode on his motorcycle I wanted one of my own."

"I didn't know you wanted to ride, doll."

"Yup. I planned on getting one when I graduated but life just kept getting in the way. Riding on the back of yours had made me get the itch again to get on one again."

"We'll get you set up this summer. Chicks who ride are hot," I winked at her in the mirror and she laughed.

"Maybe. I kind of like being on the back of yours." That sounded promising. I wasn't going to be back on my bike until April, and that was five months away.

"So what happened, doll?"

I watched her in the mirror as she ran my hair through her fingers, enjoying her touch. "Matt told me he was going to a party one night, but I had to work late, so he went by himself." Uh oh, this did not sound like it was going to end well. "I ended getting off early and decided to head out to the party he was at." She set her scissors down in front of the mirror and ran the comb through my hair. "It was one of our friends that were throwing the party. The friend had told me he had seen Matt arrive about an hour before, but he hadn't seen him in a bit. I just wandered around looking for him. Then I opened a bedroom door and walked in on two guys kissing."

"So you didn't find Matt?"

Gwen laughed and shook her head. "Oh, I found him alright. He was one of the guys who was kissing."

What the fuck! "He was bi? Did you know?"

"That would be a negative. It never once crossed my mind in five years that Matt was gay. He was the perfect bad boy. Rough around the edges with just the right amount of sweet. I'm sure his boyfriend, Juan, appreciates it." A laugh bubbled out of her, a smirk on her lips.

"So, you said you were with him for six years, but you found him with a guy a year before that."

"Yeah, about that. I was an idiot and stayed with him because he was too afraid to tell anyone."

"Pretty selfish of him to ask you to stay with him."

"It's not like he made me. It wasn't exactly a hard thing to do either. He was my best friend and my boyfriend for so long that he just stopped being my boyfriend and stayed my friend. At least for that last year." She tossed the comb in front of me and propped her hands on her hips. "All done." She unsnapped the cape and whipped it off me. She tossed in the chair she was sitting in before and watched me in the mirror.

I turned my head to the left and right, checking out what she had done. My eyes connected with hers, and I nodded my head. "Pretty fucking good, doll. You should do this full-time."

She laughed swatting me on the shoulder. "I just might do that."

She worked on cleaning the scissor and comb, putting everything back where it belonged, and I watched her. "So, you think I have this big secret that is going to push you away, right?"

"I don't know. I think I have a little self-doubt in myself, too. Paige swears she knew there was something off about Matt, but she could never put her finger on it." She turned around and leaned against the small counter in front of the mirror. "I had no indication at all until I saw Matt getting it on with another guy, that he was gay. Never saw it coming."

"Doll, you can't blame yourself for the fact that he lied to you for so long."

She shrugged her shoulders and turned back around. "I gave him everything I had, and he lied to me the whole time. I can't do that again."

"So you're never going to trust anyone again?"

"It's less painful that way."

I grabbed her hand and tugged her into my lap. She straddled my lap, and I saw there were tears in her eyes. "Doll, he's not worth your tears."

"I know that," she sniffed. "I stopped crying over him a long time ago."

"Then why the tears?"

"Because I'm afraid to love you, but I'm afraid to lose you." She wiped her eyes and smiled. "I think this is what they call being stuck between a rock and a hard place."

"Gwen, do you want to be with me?"

"Yes. Completely." Yes!

"Then stop worrying about everything else. I can promise I don't have a huge secret that no one knows that is going to rip us apart. You know about Evie, and that is something I never tell anyone."

She reached up, cupping my cheek. "I'm sorry about your sister," she whispered.

And this was why I loved Gwen. Hard as nails, but the most loving woman. "Thank you, baby." I leaned into her hand, relishing her touch. Whenever she freely touched me, it was like a small battle won. "I miss her every day, but it helped me realize I needed to live my life how I wanted because you never knew when it was going to be taken away."

"You know what you want and you take it," she smiled big, "me included."

"Yeah, doll. You are the one thing I know I want. Now, tomorrow, fifty years from now. I need you."

"I'm terrified, Gambler. Except I can't say no anymore. I say I don't want to fall in love with you when I already have."

My body went still at her words. She was crying again, but she had a huge grin on her face. She already loved me?

She already loved me.

Thank you, God.

*ʼ*ʼ*ʼ*ʼ*ʼ*ʼ*ʼ*ʼ*ʼ*ʼ*

Chapter 27

Gwen

I waited.

Then I waited some more. Gambler just stared at me, not saying a word. OK, I might regret just telling him that I loved him. Except wasn't that what he wanted me to do? Let go of worrying and just go for it. Well, I loved him.

"Now would be a good time to say something."

"Pants off, now."

I reared back, pushing against his chest and looked at him like he was crazy. "What the hell do you mean pants off? That's not exactly the thing you say to someone when they tell you they love you for the first time."

"It is when I want to be inside you the first time I say it." He bucked his hips under me, prompting me to get up. I scurried off his lap and watched as he unzipped his pants. "Ten seconds, doll."

I scrambled out of my pants because I knew the tone in his voice. Gambler wasn't playing. I loved when he talked to me like that. He knew what he wanted from me, and he was going to take it. This man drove me crazy in the best way possible.

"Shirt, too. I want to see you."

"Gambler, the damn street is right there." I dropped my pants to the floor and stepped out of them.

"Worry about me, not the damn street. Shirt, now."

I grabbed the hem and pulled it over my head. "You're crazy. Absolutely insane."

"But you love me," he smirked. He leaned forward and pulled his shirt over his head. "Hop on, doll."

Sitting in my salon chair, Gambler was naked as the day he was born with a raging hard-on. I was never going to be able to look at this chair again without blushing. I stood between his legs and reached for his dick. He may want me to climb up, but first I wanted to have my own fun. His cock was hard, throbbing and hot in my hand. I stroked him up and down as he groaned under my touch. I sunk down to my knees and licked my lips.

"Oh my fucking god," he growled as I leaned forward and slid his dick all the way to the back of my throat. "Damn, your mouth is perfect, doll."

I glanced up, my eyes connecting with his as he watched his dick disappear in and out of my mouth. My tongue stroked him as I sped up, my head bobbing up and down.

He threaded his fingers through my hair and gripped my head. He took control, setting the pace. "I'll die without you," he whispered, closing his eyes.

I swallowed as he hit the back of my throat, and he moaned low and deep. He sat forward, lifting my head up. "Ride me, now," he demanded. I stood up, and he grabbed my hips, pulling me onto his lap.

"I wanted you to cum in my mouth," I purred, grabbing his dick. I stroked him up and down, as I licked my lips, his eyes watching my every move.

"Next time, I need to be in that tight pussy."

I rose up on my knees that were on either side of his body and slowly slid down on his cock, filling me. I leaned forward, my forehead resting against Gambler's forehead. "Tell me again why I ran away from this?" I laughed.

Gambler grabbed my ass and squeezed. "Doll, right now all I can think about is how tight your pussy is around my dick. Fuck the past, this, right here," he thrust his hips up, "is all I'm worried about."

I grabbed onto his shoulders, slowly pushing myself up. "Then you forgive me?" I held myself up, just the tip of his cock in me.

"Are you withholding that pussy from me until I say yes?"

"Tell me you love me."

"No," he growled, his hands holding my hips, his fingers digging into me. "Give me that pussy."

I shook my head no, but he thrust his hips, slamming back into me. I moaned as he bottomed out, "Not fair."

"I don't see you complaining too much, doll," he gritted out. His jaw was clenched as he lifted me off then thrust up and he brought me back down. My eyes shut and my head rolled to the side as I fell into a haze of desire. He leaned forward, trailing kisses up my collar bone. "This needs to come off." He nipped at my bra, pulling the strap down with his teeth.

I reached behind me, unhooking the bra and tossed it on the floor. "You do realize anyone walking by can see me, right?" I purred, cupping my breasts as I looked out the window.

"No one is going to walk by. Eyes to me," he growled.

My eyes snapped to him and a grin spread across my lips. "You're awfully demanding."

"We've gone over this before. I'm demanding when it's something I want. Right now, I want you." He leaned forward, his mouth devouring my breast. His hands stayed on my hips, helping to move me up and down on his dick.

"Don't stop," I moaned. Gambler sped up, bouncing me up and down, grunting each time I slid back down. I grabbed onto his shoulders, steadying myself. I dug my knees into the chair and held on.

"Say it," he growled.

"No," I moaned. I tossed my head back, moaning as he took me closer and closer to the edge with each thrust.

"Tell me you love me."

I shook my head no, unable to talk. I don't know how Gambler did it, but each time he took me, it was better than the last.

"I'm gonna cum, doll. Tell me," he demanded.

"I love you!" I cried as I tipped over the edge, drowning in Gambler.

"I love you. I'll love you till the day I die," he gritted out, his teeth clenched. He had thrust three more times before he cried out, filling me with his cum. "Mine," he chanted over and over.

I collapsed forward, resting my head on his shoulder. "That was fucking amazing," I breathed out.

Gambler thrust one last time, holding me tight and staying buried deep inside me. "I love you," he whispered into my ear.

I wrapped my arms around his shoulders and cried my eyes out. I cried for the girl so many years ago who had her heart broken and never really healed. I cried for the simple fact that I finally felt like I had found a place that felt like home. And I cried for the sheer fact that I had found the man who was going to be everything I thought didn't exist. "I love you, too."

"You're crying all over me, doll," Gambler laughed. I sat back, pushing against his chest. He reached up and wiped every tear that fell away. "No crying, Gwen. I love you."

"I couldn't get you to say it and now you won't shut up," I laughed.

He shrugged his shoulders and smirked. "It sounds pretty good coming out of my mouth. You're probably going to hear it all the time now."

"Promise?" I whispered, pressing a kiss to his lips.

"At least fifty times a day, doll."

"I guess that's just something I'll have to get used to." I laid my head back on his shoulders, this time smiling and not bawling my eyes out.

"You think you could get one of these chairs for my room? That was the best sex I've ever had. Well, except for that one night you woke me up with your mouth, and then I took you against the wall three hours ago."

"These chairs are over two thousand dollars. I think we'll have to come here if you want to do that again." Headlights flashed through the window, and I scooted down Gambler's lap, ducking.

"Doll, they can't see you," he laughed, wrapping his arms around me. My stomach growled loud, and I looked Gambler right in the eye. "Am I supposed to ignore that?" He asked, smirking.

"No," I laughed. "I can't help it I'm starving. I didn't grab anything to eat when I left, and all I did was inventory the past two hours."

"See, that's what you get when you run away from me."

"Hungry?" I laughed.

"Yes, exactly. How about we each throw our clothes on, and I'll run down the street and order Chinese while you shut down the shop."

"Sounds like a solid plan." I pushed against Gambler, trying to stand up but he didn't let me go. "Let me up. Can you not hear my stomach sounding like a beluga whale?"

"Yeah, doll, I hear it," he laughed. "First, I'm gonna need something for you."

"Hmm, I bet I know what it is."

"Oh yeah, you think you're really ready to bet against me again? I did just collect from you two times."

I crossed my arms over my chest and glared at him. "Trust me, I remember."

"Well, how about no more bets anymore, at least for a bit. I just placed a huge wager on a longshot, and I thankfully won."

"Oh yeah, what did you win?" I had a feeling I was going to have to keep an eye on Gambler and all his betting in the future. Although it did seem that he won most of his bets. I wonder what he bet on that he won now.

"You. You were my longshot bet, doll. I came here tonight, and I had no idea what the hell was going to go on. All I knew was that I couldn't stay away from you any longer."

"So, I'm your winnings?"

"Yeah, doll. You were my most risky bet, but the most rewarding."

I leaned forward, my lips brushing against his. "Thank god you're a betting man." Gambler threaded his fingers through my hair, pressing his lips to mine and gave me everything in that one kiss.

Someone I could trust, love, have fun with and have the best sex ever with. If you asked me, we were both winners in that longshot bet.

''*'*'*'*'*'*'*'*'*

Chapter 28

Gwen

I had just put everything away from Gambler's haircut when I heard a noise in the back. Gambler had left ten minutes ago to grab the food, and I hadn't expected him back yet.

I looked out the front window of the shop, glancing up and down the street but didn't see anything. I figured it must have just been something settling back in the storeroom and brushed it off.

My phone ding in my pocket, and I pulled it out, seeing Meg had texted me. I plopped down in the salon chair Gambler and I had used and opened up the text message.

You and Gambler make up and have wild monkey sex yet? Leave it to Meg to get straight to the point.

We're all good.

But did you have wild monkey sex?

I'm not answering that. Meg cracked me up.

You guys soooo had wild monkey sex.

Is there a reason for you texting me other than talking about hot monkey sex?

Yeah. Oh, my God. I laughed at her one-word response. She was a straight up nut.

And that would be?????

You wanna be a bridesmaid?

Really? Me? Wow, I didn't expect her to ask me that. I had only known her for a couple of months, although I did feel really close to her and all the other the girls.

Yes, you. The wedding is New Year's Eve by the way. What?!?! New Year's Eve? That was just over a month away.

This New Years?

Yes, you think Lo is going to wait over a year? He said Christmas, I countered with New Year's Eve.

Holy Cow! That's awesome! Yes, I'll be your bridesmaid!

Sweet. I'll let you get back to sweaty monkey sex. TTYL

Wow, Meg and King were getting married. Hell yes! And, I got to be a bridesmaid. Plus, now I get to get all dolled- I whirled around in my chair when I heard something fall in the back. What the fuck was that?

I heard the click of a gun being cocked and froze. "Throw your phone on the floor and slowly turn around." I couldn't see anyone, but I knew they had to be in the back room. I tossed my phone on the floor and slowly turned in my chair.

"We've waited a long time for those Knights to leave one of their women alone. Although you're not the one we want." The man walked out of the shadows of the back hall, and he held a gun pointed directly at me.

I clasped my hands in my lap and prayed for Gambler to come back. "How... how did...did you... get in... here?" I stuttered. I was petrified with fear.

"You need better locks around here. Anyone could get in." He walked closer to me and I knew right away he was part of the Assassins.

"Please don't hurt me," I whispered as he walked closer, only a few feet away from me.

"I'm not here to hurt you. I'm here to give you a message."

I nodded my head, unable to talk. If he wasn't going to hurt me, then why the hell did he have a gun pointed at me?

He sat in the chair across from me, the gun still trained on me. "Do you know who you hang around?" I shook my head, no, not knowing the right answer to the question. "They're murderers," he spat out. "That is who you decide to spend your time with."

I had no idea what he was talking about, and I honestly didn't want to know. As much as I didn't want to believe that anyone with the Devil's Knights was a murderer, I knew that if they did have to do anything like what this guy was saying, the person deserved it. I had spent time with everyone in that club and there was no way that I was wrong about this. The Devil's Knights were not murderers. "If that's what you believe."

"They are!" He yelled at me. He waved the gun at me, his hand shaking. His eyes flared with anger, and I knew I hadn't said the right thing.

"OK," I whispered.

"Damn right, but you want to know who we're going after and destroy?" I just stared at him, waiting for him to continue. "Rigid. Rigid is the one who went after my cousin and took him away from my family. Rigid is the one I am going to destroy." He stood up, standing right in front of me. He leaned down, his face an inch away from me. "You tell Rigid and all those Knights you think that are going to keep you safe, I'm coming for his woman and his niño."

I gasped at his words. Not only terrified for myself right now, but for Cyn and her baby, too. I knew Rigid would die before anything would happen to Cyn. But the man who was standing in front of me seemed like one crazy fucker.

"Stand up," he ordered, waving the gun at me. I stood up, my legs shaking underneath me. "Move." He nodded to the back of the shop. He shoved the gun into my back, prompting me to walk.

"Please don't hurt Cyn," I pleaded as we walked.

"Stupid woman, you have no idea what they've done. My cousin died because of that puta." We stopped in front of the bathroom and he pushed me inside. "Make sure you deliver my message." He slammed the door shut, but he didn't move away. I listened, trying to hear what he was doing. He stomped to the left and then I heard something being dragged on the floor, scraping it. Something slammed against the bathroom door and I screamed. "No getting out, puta," he sneered. I heard him move to the back door and then silence.

I tried pushing the door open, but it was blocked by my file cabinet he had pushed in front of the door. Shit. I pounded on the door, hoping Gambler was back, but he wasn't. Double shit.

I leaned against the door and slid down, wrapping my arms around my knees. My mind was whirling with everything the guy had told me. I couldn't believe that King and all the guys were murderers. I held my head in my hands and ran my fingers through my hair.

I went over everything the guy had told me and my blood boiled at the thought of him hurting Cyn and her baby. I had known that Cyn's ex had hurt her, but I never really got all the details of what happened.

I leaned my head against the door and sighed. The only thing I could do right now is wait for Gambler and get the answers to all my questions then. I just hoped Cyn was going to be OK until I told Gambler the message.

Come on, Gambler. I need you.

''*'*'*'*'*'*'*'*'*'*

Chapter 29

GAMBLER

"Soy sauce or anything else I can help you with?"

"No, I'm fine," I turned away from the counter and walked over to the storefront window. If I had known that fucking Cherry worked here, I would have told Gwen she was going to have to be hungry till we went somewhere else to eat.

"I haven't been able to make it out to the clubhouse lately. I've heard the parties aren't happening as much anymore."

I glanced over my shoulder to see Cherry come out from behind the counter and lean against it. I couldn't believe I use to think this chick was hot. Now she just looked slutty and wore out. "We've become more selective about who comes to the club." I turned back around and watched the traffic drive by. It was more interesting than talking to Cherry.

"Hmm, I bet King's girlfriend has something to do with that."

I shrugged my shoulders, not wanting to give her the satisfaction of talking about Meg. Meg, Cyn, and Cherry all hated each other. Cyn's asshat of an ex was Cherry's brother who had met an untimely end at the hands of Rigid and the club.

"I don't know why he would settle for-"

"Is my food done?" I cut her off, not wanting to hear her bitch fest about Meg. Cherry was delusional if she thought that King was going to leave Meg for her.

Cherry glared at me and thankfully didn't continue. "I'll go check," she snarled.

I sighed, wondering what the hell we were all thinking to have Cherry in the clubhouse. Thankfully I had never tapped that, but I knew some of the other brothers weren't that lucky to say that. Demon being one of them.

Cherry yelled in the back, asking about the food and I smirked. The last we had known, Cherry was working at the plant that Meg and Cyn worked at. Obviously, things hadn't worked out there and now she was slinging Chinese food.

I looked down the street toward the salon and watched a black van slowly drive by. A Mexican man was driving and he watched me as he slowly cruised by, a snarl on his lips. He spit out the window at me and took off once he passed the restaurant.

I pulled my phone out of my pocket and called Gwen. It rang until her voicemail picked up. I instantly ended the call and hit send again. Still no answer. Something wasn't right. I ripped open the door and ran down the street to the shop.

The phone was pressed to my ear as I called the shop, thinking she might not hear her cell ringing. I skidded at the door of the shop and heard the phone ringing but didn't see Gwen anywhere in the shop.

"Yo!" I turned around and saw Demon pull up to the curb.

"Gwen's not answering the phone," I yelled, yanking on the door. It was still locked so I grabbed my keys and quickly opened the door. I heard Demon slam his door behind me and run across the street.

"I got your back," he said. He pulled a gun out of the waistband of his jeans and looked up and down the street. "I've been driving around and haven't seen anything, but that don't mean shit." He nodded at me to go in, and I pulled the door open.

"Gwen!" I called, looking around. Nothing seemed to be out of place, but that didn't mean nothing was wrong.

"I'm gonna walk around to the back," Demon ducked out the door and slinked around the side of the building.

"Gwen!" I called again. I walked forward, kicking something on the floor. It skidded across the ground, hitting the wall. I reached down, picked it up and realized it was Gwen's phone.

"Gambler!" I heard a door bang against something as she called for me.

I headed to the back room and saw a file cabinet pushed up against the door. "What the fuck?" I shoved the cabinet out of the way and Gwen threw open the door of the bathroom and threw her arms around me.

"What the fuck happened?" I asked as I ran my hands all over her body.

"I was texting Meg, and then I heard something fall in the backroom. I turned around and a guy was standing there, pointing a gun at me."

Rage boiled inside me as soon as I heard he was pointing a gun at her. "Did he say who he was?"

She shook her head no and leaned back, "No, he was a short guy and Mexican. He said I needed to tell you he is coming for Cyn and her baby. He kept calling everyone in the Knights murderers."

I gritted my teeth and knew exactly who was just here. "Fucking Big A. He's not sending his minions to take care of shit anymore. He came himself."

"He was infuriated, Gambler. He said the Knights were going to pay for killing his cousin. He asked me if I knew you were all murderers."

Her body quaked in my arms and I held her tighter. I buried my face in her hair. "I'm so sorry I wasn't here, doll. I'm so sorry."

She sniffled, wiping her nose on my shoulder. "It's not your fault, Gambler. I'm just worried. He didn't hurt me this time, but he seemed so desperate. It was like his eyes were filled with hate and anger."

We figured the assassins were getting more desperate, especially when they went after Gwen and me before, but I don't think we knew what kind of crazy we were dealing with. "Did he hurt you anywhere?"

"No, he just kept the gun on me the whole time. He shoved me into the bathroom, but that didn't hurt. He just scared me more than anything. I don't know how he got in."

"He busted the lock on the back door." Gwen and I both turned around to see Demon walk in, the broken handle in his hand. "I should have walked around the building when I showed up before, Gwen. This is all my fault."

Demon was right, he should have checked things out, but I probably would have done the same thing if I were him. He could see her through the glass the whole time so there really wasn't a point to walk around the building. "It's not your fault, brother. I didn't think he would go after Gwen either. I'm sure he's been waiting for us to leave one of the girls alone and Gwen just happened to be the unlucky one."

Gwen was still wrapped up in my arms, turned sideways. "Even if you would have done a walk around, I don't think you would have saw it, Demon. I had heard a noise before he came in, but I didn't think anything of it."

"Why didn't you call me when you heard the noise?"

"Because I thought it was something settling or something in the back. I had just moved everything around for inventory. I wasn't thinking that it was someone breaking in. I've known all along the Assassins were a problem, but I thought that I was on the sidelines, not important to them."

"Well, I think after this, it's safe to say that no one is safe." Demon dropped the door handle in the garbage and pulled his phone out. "I'll give King a heads up and then we can work on securing that door before we head back." Demon walked back out the door, leaving it open.

"I'm sorry I didn't call you. The noise wasn't that loud so I just ignored it."

"You're fine, doll." She shivered in my arms and laid her head on my shoulder. "I'm pretty sure I saw him leaving. I was standing at the window of the Chinese place when a black van rolled by."

"This is all so crazy, Gambler." She tilted her head back and looked me in the eye. "He said Rigid killed his cousin, did he?" Her gorgeous eyes looked up at me, needing answers.

"Anything I say to you, Gwen, stays between us. That includes not telling Meg, Cyn or Marley. I have no idea what they know, but I don't want them finding out from you."

"I promise I won't say anything."

I ran my fingers through my hair and walked her over to the chair we were sitting in earlier. I pulled her into my lap and she curled up, wrapping her arms around my neck. "Do you know what happened to Cyn?"

"Not the details. I know she lost her baby."

"She lost her baby because her asshat of an ex beat the hell out of her when she told him she was pregnant. They were already broken up because he was cheating on her the whole time."

"Oh my God, poor, Cyn."

"Yeah, doll. She went through some shit after that. Her ex knew he fucked up and went to his cousin Big A, the guy who was here tonight, and helped him hide. Troy found him, then Rigid and the rest of the club paid him a visit."

"Did… did you help?" she stuttered, her eyes huge.

I brushed the hair out of her face and pressed a kiss to the side of her head. "I was there, doll. I had to be there for my brother."

She buried her face in my chest and wrapped her arms around my neck. "He hurt Cyn and took away her baby," she whispered.

"He did."

"He deserved what he got."

"We're not murderers, doll. But when someone hurts someone we love, we take matters into our own hands."

She trailed her hand up my chest and cupped my cheek. She lifted her head, my lips a breath away from her's. "You wronged a right. You did what needed to be done," she whispered.

"We couldn't let him get away with it."

She nodded her head yes and threaded her fingers through my hair. "I love you, Gambler."

I slammed my lips down on her's, not knowing what to say. I love you didn't seem to fit what I was feeling for Gwen. My chest felt like it was going to explode, and all I wanted to do was bury myself in Gwen. There had never been anything in my life that had ever made me feel this way. "I love you more than anything in this world," I growled against her lips.

"You know people are going to think we're crazy for falling in love so fast," she laughed.

"I could give a shit what people think. As long as you're happy I don't care."

"Yo!" Demon called, walking back into the shop. "King said he doesn't want to tell the girls right now, especially Cyn."

"We have to tell Cyn, he said he's coming for her." Gwen jumped out of her chair and put her hands on her hips.

"Doll, relax." Gwen glared at me but didn't say anything else.

"Right now, only Gwen is to know about what happened. Rigid isn't going to let Cyn out of his sight, and she'll always have two other club members with her including Rigid. King isn't going to let anything happen to her." Demon walked over to the front desk and started searching through the drawers. "You got a tool box or something, babe? We need to get that door fixed for the night."

"It's in the back, but we're not done talking about keeping this from the girls, especially Cyn."

Demon crouched down and pulled out a roll of duct tape. "Yeah, we are done talking about it, babe, because it's club business. That's what King wants, and that's what is going to happen. If you want to tell the girls, you will not only have Gambler to deal with, but King also. Meg may make him look like a teddy bear, but I can guarantee you that he is not."

"I'm not part of the club, I don't have to listen to him." She stomped her foot as Demon walked by.

"No, you don't, but you're dating a member of the club. You think King wants you to not tell the girls for the hell of it. He's doing it to protect them." Demon shook his head and walked into the backroom.

"This is bullshit," she hissed at me.

"Gwen, knock it off. It's not like you have to lie to them. Just don't tell them. I really doubt King is going to keep this away from them for that long."

"I don't like this at all." She crossed her arms over her chest and glared at me. "Damn, Meg just asked me to be in her wedding and now I have to lie to her."

"Gwen, for the damn fifth time, it's not lying. Don't. Tell. Her." Jesus. Gwen had barely known Meg and the girls, but she was rather fiercely protective of them.

"I'm giving you one week to tell them before I do."

Gwen's attitude was out ten-fold tonight. "Two weeks and then you can say something. I'm not arguing with you over this."

"What if King wanted me to keep a secret from you, would you be OK with that?"

"No, because that is different than this. I'm a part of the club and King wouldn't keep this away from me. The only

248

reason you know is because you were involved in it. I'm not going to say it again. Let it drop."

"Gambler, I just think-"

"Gwen! Stop, now." I ordered.

She stopped mid-sentence and I swear to God she growled.

Oh shit.

''*'*'*'*'*'*'*'*

Chapter 30

Gwen

One kick to the nuts and I'd have him on his knees. One kick.

I couldn't believe that I was going to have to keep this from Meg, Cyn, and Marley. I worked every day with Marley. We talked all the time. He didn't think that something like this was going to come up. The only reason I was going to agree not to tell the girls was because Cyn didn't need the extra stress right now since she wasn't very far along in her pregnancy. "Two weeks, and then I'm letting it out," I vowed, holding up two fingers.

"Two weeks. I bet before that King will have already told them. He just needs some time to figure some shit out first. I promise."

Hmph. I wasn't happy, but I understood where King was coming from. "Fine," I pouted, crossing my arms over my chest.

"Thank you, doll." He walked over and wrapped me up in a hug. I may love this man but that didn't mean I had to agree with everything he said. I knew with him being connected to the club that there were going to be times where he couldn't tell me things, but I didn't think that I would have to keep secrets. "I love you," he mumbled into my hair.

"I love you, too, Gambler. Hey," I said, pulling back, "what's your real name?"

"Just call me Gambler, doll. Only my mom calls me by my real name, and I hate it."

"No, you're going to have to tell me. You promised no secrets."

Gambler sighed, and I knew I got him. "It's Anthony."

"Anthony? Tony?" I smirked. He didn't look like an Anthony, but I could totally see calling him Tony.

"Gambler, doll. Just Gambler."

I leaned forward, whispering in his ear. "Can I call you Anthony when you're pounding into me, making me cum?"

"I'm pretty sure at that point, doll, with my dick buried inside you, I'll answer to Edgar or anything else you want to call me."

"Oh, I know! How about I call you Antonio in a Spanish accent. Oh, Antonio!" I shouted, throwing my head back.

"What the fuck are you two doing?" Demon asked. We both turned around to see Demon standing there, my neon pink tool box in his hand. "Who the fuck is Antonio?"

Gambler busted out laughing and pulled me close. "Nobody you know, brother."

"Let's get this shit done so we can get back to the clubhouse. King is waiting for us." Demon headed out the back and started banging on the door.

"Demon sure does like to boss you around."

"He's the VP, doll. He can." Gambler slid his arm around my shoulders and walked me over to the front desk. "Get your shit ready while Demon and I take care of the door. I've got your phone in my pocket." He pulled it out and handed it to me.

"Thanks. I just need to go to the bathroom and grab my purse." He leaned in, pressing a kiss to my lips and headed out back to help Demon.

"About fucking time you rip yourself away from her." I heard Demon grumble. I shook my head and headed to the bathroom. I glimpsed Gambler helping Demon as I walked into the bathroom and he threw a wink at me. I blushed, my face turning red and slammed the door shut behind me when I heard Demon cussing at Gambler for not paying attention when he had swung the hammer, nailing Demon on the thumb.

I had never really spent much time with Demon before, but I never knew he was such a crank ass. He definitely needed to get laid.

I looked in the mirror, fluffing my hair and laughed. What a day. A bride from hell, fighting with Gambler, making up with Gambler, held at gunpoint (the definite downfall of my day), fighting with Gambler again, and then we made up.

I had a feeling from here on out that was going to be how my days would go. Well, minus the being held at gunpoint. Gambler and I might go at it, arguing and pressing each other's buttons, but when we made up, boy did we make up.

"Doll, you ready?" Gambler hollered.

I grinned at myself in the mirror, never looking happier.

Was I ready?

You bet your ass I was ready for whatever life had in store for me as long as Gambler was with me.

He said he had never bet on such a longshot before, but the same could be said for me.

I whirled around as the door opened and Gambler stood on the other side, smirking at me. "Just looking at yourself in the mirror, doll?"

Such a smart ass. I reached up, threading my fingers through his hair and kissed him with everything I had. I loved this man and nothing could come between us. He bet on me, won, and now I was his forever.

Win, win.

''*'*'*'*'*'*'*'*'*'*

Chapter 31

Meg

One hour.

One fucking hour.

Lo had left our bed over an hour ago after he got a phone call. I asked him, as he was hopping back into his jeans and boots, what the hell was going on. All he told me was he had some club shit to take care of. I had glanced at the clock, seeing it was ten o'clock and wondered what kind of club business he would have then.

I had grabbed my phone and shot a message off to Cyn, seeing if Rigid was gone, too, but she never responded. She had probably passed out as soon as her head had hit the pillow. She was only a couple of months along, but that baby seemed to be draining all of her energy.

I swung my legs out of bed, my feet hitting the cold hardwood floor, and a chill ran through me. I turned on the bedside lamp and the light bounced off my ring, making it sparkle. I held my hand up, moving my finger in the light, watching the light dance and smiled.

December thirty-first I was going to marry the man I loved. Lo hadn't believed that I had agreed to get married that soon, but I figured how much could things change if we got married? I loved him and he loved me, Remy, and Blue. What more could a girl want?

"You still up, babe?" Lo asked, walking through the door.

"When you're used to working and staying up till eleven o'clock every night, Lo, you tend to stay up late even if you're not working."

"What's with the sass, babe?" He asked as he shut the door, locking it behind him and pulled his shirt over his head.

God dammit Lo looked good. We had just got done having sex when the phone had ringed, and I already wanted him again. "The sass, as you call it, has to do with the fact that you got a phone call, didn't tell me what the hell was going on and left."

"I told you it was club business."

"I don't care if it's club business. I've watched Sons of Anarchy, Jax told Tara shit."

Lo busted out laughing and shook his head at me. "You do realize that is a TV show and not real life, right?"

I waved my hand at him, not wanting to get into the same fight we always had when I brought up Sons. "Whatever, that's not the point. The point is that you're not telling me what the hell is going on."

"Meg, I don't need to tell you what is going on. It has to do with the club and that is where it's going to stay. I'm not talking about this anymore." He unbuttoned his pants, tossed them on the back of the desk chair and climbed into bed.

"Is anyone hurt?"

Lo sighed and grabbed my pillow, smashing it behind his head. Bastard always stole my pillow but he let me sleep and drool on him every night. It was a good compromise. "No one is hurt."

"Does it have to do with the Banachi's?" I knew Lo had helped Leo move his sister in today so it might be a possibility that something had come up with them.

"No, nothing to do with Leo."

Damn. I was running out of things to guess. "The Assassins?"

"Meg, I'm not playing twenty questions with you. I'm damn tired and right now, all I want to do is turn on the TV, watch a movie, and sleep."

This wasn't working. I switched off the light and slid back under the covers. "I'm sorry you're tired, hunny," I purred, running my hand up his bare chest.

Lo grabbed my hand and pulled me on top of him. "As much as I like you touching me, babe, I'm not going to tell you what the hell is going on." We were nose to nose, and I could tell that I really wasn't going to get anywhere with Lo. At least not tonight. "I promise that everything will be fine, you just need to trust me."

"Fine," I whispered, laying down on top of him. "Can I, at least, pick what movie we are going to watch?"

"Anything you want, babe," he laughed.

"Put on Mad Max." Lo reached over, grabbing the remote of the nightstand and started the DVD that was already in the machine.

"You do know this is the third time we've watched this movie in two weeks, right?" He asked as the opening previews started to play.

"I know. I just like it." I rolled off Lo, settling under his arm and rested my head on his shoulder.

I watched the movie mindlessly, not actually paying attention to what was going on. I glanced up at Lo, his eyes already at half mast, ready to sleep then glanced at my ring.

I was getting married in less than six weeks, and my fiancée was keeping secrets from me. From what I could tell, one of them was a dousey.

Now, I just needed to figure out how to get it out of him and then marry his sexy ass. It looked like the next six weeks were going to be busy.

''*'*'*'*'*'*'*'*

Lo

Shit.

The End

for now....

257

Coming Soon

Downshift: Skid Row Kings Series, Book 1

May 2016

They're the Kings of the street, and every King needs his Queen.

Has Luke met his match with Violet?

Keeping Meg: Devil's Knights Series, Book 6

June, 2016

They know their forever is with each other, but there's bound to be some bumps in the road to the alter.

About the Author

Winter Travers is a devoted wife, mother, and aunt turned author. With stories always flowing around her, Loving Lo was the one story that had to get out (new ones are knocking on the door daily now).

Winter loves to bake and cook when she isn't at work, zipping around on her forklift. She also has an addiction to anything MC related, her dog Thunder, and Mexican food (Tamales!)

Winter has eight books total planned for The Devil's Knights Series. Books 1, 2, 3, 4 & 5. (Loving Lo, Finding Cyn, Gravel's Road, Battling Troy and Gambler's Longshot) are available now. Book 6, Keeping Meg will be out June, 2016.

Downshift will be the first book in The Skid Row Kings Series, releasing May 2016.

Made in the USA
Charleston, SC
14 February 2016